JAKE'S PAGE

JAKE'S PAGE

A SHORT STORY & PLAY

EMILY CRAVEN

Craven Publishing

Australian Edition

Contents

Contact

Facebook: *http://www.facebook.com/EmilyCravenAuthor*

Website (bookmark me!): *http://www.cravenstories.com*

Twitter: *@cravenstories*

Instagram: *@imagesforjoy*

My Email: emily (at) cravenstories (dot) com

Other Books by Emily Craven

Original Fantasy: A Practical Guide To Writing Genre

Madeline Cain: The Adventure Begins

The Grand Adventures of Madeline Cain

Madeline Cain: Adventures In Fashion

E-Book Revolution: The Ultimate Guide to Ebook Success

To Alex

Wherever you are

Introduction

Any young person who has set foot in a University College knows that they have entered Planet Crazy within the first few hours of being covered in eggs, flour and fish sauce. It is the place the out-of-towner turns to if they want two hundred instant (Asylum certified) friends. On the surface the heritage listed buildings and formal black-robed dinners would persuade parents this is a centre of learning and support. But then one college steals all the forks from the college up the road and it's on! In an instant the calm, studious high-school student becomes a Collegian to whom no dare, drinking game or sport is out of bounds. Everyday life becomes an adventure, and college becomes a platform from which a young adult can recreate themselves.

Similarly, these days the truth and the "truth" about who you are, are at war on every social media site this side of the first world nations. You can recreate yourself from a boarder-line OCD bubble boy to a tree hugging hippy with a few select page likes, status updates and pictures of suspicious bong-like glassware. Anyone who has frequented Facebook would know that finding someone who doesn't stretch the truth about themselves is about as rare as a model that eats McDonalds. While many of us may stretch the truth (or at the very least only display our shinny sides) it is still amazing the picture you build up of a person through their newsfeed on your favourite social media site.

I did not appreciate this fact until my final year of college when a first year collegian, a type one diabetic, fell into a coma and died. I found out through Facebook, the majority of college found out through Facebook, his best friend found out through Facebook. And it was on Facebook that the outpourings of grief, both public and private, found a home.

The event stewed in the back of my mind, I did not know the guy, but somehow having lived in the same place and attended the same events I felt I should have. However, years later when I looked up his Facebook page (still active today) I found I did know enough about him to determine all of his personality wasn't there. There were events, people, photographs; a bundle of information in my head that complimented the online avatar. It was as though I were looking at a half person. On the flip side, I learnt a lot about who he was and how he interacted with friends that I never knew.

This brings me to the reason why I decided to fictionalise this story and why it is told in two different formats. I wanted to examine not only how teenagers use the social media platform, but how they presented themselves on Facebook in comparison to how they acted in the real world. Because there were two sides to this story and the personality of this boy: the character he presented on Facebook and his actual personality in the flesh. I felt both perspectives were important, a 2D perspective and 3D perspective as it were. In the end I conceded that they couldn't be told at once or even in the same format. They were two separate stories and they needed the right medium to be told.

Thus 'Jake's Page: A Short Story' and 'Jake's Page: A Play' were born. The short story, written first, deals with the wacky character of Jake as seen through his Facebook page and private messages. You will notice just how easy it is to get a sense of his personality through the posts he makes and the pages he 'likes'. The writing of the play required the adaption of the short story into a script, where the action of the real world could be contrasted with the posts of the digital. The adaption was completed under the mentorship of playwright Caroline Reid and focused on translating the phenomenon of Facebook to the stage, bringing the contrasts of the digital and real world to light, and delving into the reasoning behind why Jake acted as he did when he knew the risks, something we couldn't know from reading his Facebook page.

Each format tells a different story and gives us an alternate perspective into the comic personality of Jake, University life and the tragic consequences of not looking after yourself.

It is my hope that this story not only entertains and makes you laugh, but it makes you think.

Warmly,

Emily

Jake's Page: A Short Story

Jake Black　　　*[+1 Add Friend]*

*Studied Mechanical Engineering at **University of Adelaide** Lives in **Adelaide, South Australia.** From **Hobart, Tasmania.** * Born on 05 March 1989.

———————

Jake and **Tim Hand** are now friends. [Add Tim as a friend]

10 more similar stories.

Tim Hand Dear Facebook, just wait, one day they'll abandon you as well, Sincerely MySpace... Why are we here again? What's wrong with Myspace? *Posted 28th February 2008 at 11:30* [Comment * Like]

> **Jake Black** Because you decided to stay behind on the Island of the devil while I party it up at uni. Also, Facebook is the bomb!!!!!*Posted 28th February 2008 at 11:45* [Comment * Like]

> **Tim Hand** No, I'm the bomb, Facebook is the devil. *Posted 28th February 2008 at 11:58* [Comment * Like]

> **Jake Black** Don't be such a grandpa!!!! *Posted 28th February 2008 at 12:00* [Comment * Like]

> **Tim Hand** Fine. I'll stay on Facebook, but only if you take a minimalist approach to exclamation marks... *Posted 28th February 2008 at 12:07* [Comment * Like]

> **Jake Black** Done. *Posted 28th February 2008 at 12:12* [Comment * Like]

Jake joined the group **Melbourne is a backwater, but Adelaide's a city with balls!** [Join this group]

Finally!   [New Message]

[Back to messages * Delete]

Between **Katie Black** and **You.**

Katie Black *01ˢᵗ March 2008 at 22:00* [Report]

Let's face it; I couldn't wait to see the back of your face. But then you didn't turn around and wave to me when you went through the gate. Which is completely unfair! I'm the nice one in this brother-sister relationship; you should have been bawling your eyes out while I merrily kicked you on the plane. Way to ruin the fantasy.

Jake Black *01ˢᵗ March 2008 at 23:00*

Just stay out of trouble drama queen. Miss your face.

Katie Black *02ⁿᵈ March 2008 at 12:00* [Report]

You're impossible.

Tim Hand <u>poked you</u> [Poke * Ignore]

Tim Hand <u>threw a cow at your car</u> [Throw back! * Ignore]

Tim Hand <u>stuffed ice-cream down your pants</u> [Slap Tim! * Ignore]

   Confirmation You wish to slap Tim? [Slap! * I Have Changed My Mind]

   Confirmation Your slap has been sent. [Ok]

Jake and **Kyle Vanders** have joined the groups **Boags Appreciation Society** and **The Drunken Text Appreciation Society** [Join this group]

Jake likes **Triple J** [Like this page]

NOTES > My Notes   [Write a note]

Would I Be Wearing THIS If I Was Lying?

By **Jake Black The Great.** Wednesday, 5 March 2008 at 13:00.

Ok, first of all, mum, I want to say I did NOT dress myself like this. It was a dare. A dare I did not exactly say yes to, but then I was not exactly *asked* in the first place. I was ambushed. According to the college's rule book (a very *fluid* guide) it was a completely legal, to-be-expected O-Week requirement known as Drop-Offs. I mean, it's definitely expected that your locked door will open at 6am and you will be held down while some senior collegian uses you as a canvas, then removes your money and phone and bundles you into the boot of a car. Right? Right??

You've got to give Duncan credit, it took most people in Handorf (our local 'German' town) ages to realise the lederhosen was painted on and not real clothing. I think the buckles super glued to my nipples were the main perpetrator of *that* illusion. But once they realised I was wearing just a g-string and that my bum was in fact real and bared to the world, not enclosed in super tight pants, then I got 'the look'.

You know the one. Parents judge you as the drunken/ sexual/ mad/ irresponsible/ disrespectful deviant that you are and the girls try to take a closer look at your junk. Then they tut, or laugh and suddenly paint can do everything other then hid how very, very naked you are. It was awesome!

I was better off then Amanda, who let's face it, got the raw end of the stick on this one. She was dressed as the Bible's very own Eve with some skimpy plastic leaves on a very small bikini. Try explaining *that* to the class of 5 year olds taking a walk on the main street. I think the teacher was expecting her to give a lap dance on one of the light poles the way she hurried the wide-eyed midgets away. Amanda's got balls though, the way she walked through that town you'd think she dressed like this all the time. If only she didn't keep snapping my g-string and giving the game away.

Trying to get out of the Adelaide Hills without a phone or a wallet… well, not quite as awesome as scaring off young children. It is a *long* walk to Adelaide; try hailing a car when you look like a homeless person who paints himself rather than buying pants. Damn near impossible.

Besides we were in a race. Everything at college is a race or competition. Who can scull beer the fastest, get drunk the fastest, finish an exam with the least words and still get a pass, win the most sporting comps, find the most yeti's, create the most mayhem at another college. It was a race I wanted to win! If I didn't, then all those tourist photographs I was now in would have been for nothing. After failing to flag down ten edgy drivers and one errant horse rider, we decided that by then we were shameless enough to try talking ourselves onto the public transport system.

"So what do we tell them?" I asked Amanda.

"We're part of a travelling circus?" She tried.

"Ah…"

"We're fringe buskers? Victims of a practical joke? Spreading the word of the Lord?"

"Got mugged at a yodelling competition?"

Amanda sniggered, snapping my g-string, "You got more than mugged mate."

"Do you think we'll get more sympathy if we tell them we got drunk, or the truth?"

"In my experience, no-one has sympathy for drunks. Besides, the truth is more of a challenge."

I don't think the bus would have stopped if there wasn't an old lady sitting at the stop with us. That was one of the more awkward conversations I've had in my life. ("In my day, they use to do that sort of thing in private. ") The once-plucky Amanda was overcome with a sudden bout of muteness and shoved me in front of her as we stepped up to the driver.

The driver looked me up and down with the most peculiar expression I've ever seen. It was the look of someone who was caught at the tipping point between extreme horror and hysterical laughter. "Explain," was all he could manage. So we explained. "You expect me to believe, that around 50 teenagers are dressed like this every year and dropped off all around Adelaide, without a single fight to keep your clothes on? Without a single hidden dollar up the who-ha?"

"There's not much fighting you can do when you're in a car boot, even one as roomy as ours," I replied. "Seriously mate, would I be wearing THIS if I was lying?"

"Kid, I don't want to hazard a guess at what you do in your private time. But if I see you out here again in anything less than snow gear, I'm going to run you over with this bus. Now hide yourself in a corner where the other passengers can't see you and NO shenanigans."

At least our jaunt in Handorf prepared us for the reception we received walking through the city. Even the buskers stared. And to top it all off we lost! To a couple of goons in ninja outfits who convinced mounted police to give them a ride back to college.

As a side note, does anyone have a good method for removing superglue from skin?

[Comment * Like * Share]

Katie Black and **3 others** like this.

Amanda Pickup We were soooo much better off then Kyle from the US. They drove him all the way to the Kangaroo Island Ferry, dressed in a tutu and leotard, put him on the boat and told him he was going to New Zealand. He flipped! PS. Have you tried being a man, Special Boy, and ripping it off? *Posted 12hrs ago* [Comment * Like]

> **Jake Black** Bahaha! At least our bus driver didn't keep licking his lips like Andy's guy. Did Andy tell you he hitched a ride in a lorry and drove it for two hours while the truckie had a sleep in the back? And how about I superglue those plastic leafs to you and see how well you do? *Posted 11hrs ago* [Comment * Like]

Tim Hand Dude is that a *Goon box* on your head? No wonder the oldies thought you were drunk! Did you have to drink that before or after they duct tapped it to your head? Were you playing that Goon of Fortune game I've been hearing about? It ok, you can tell me. Or PM me. *Posted 4hrs ago* [Comment * Like]

> **Jake Black** Dude, let's just say a box was the least of my problems. Have you ever tried getting the smell of lobster out of your hair when it's been strapped there for six hours in 35 degree heat? *Posted 4hrs ago* [Comment * Like]

> **Katie Black** Timothy, it's Jakey's mother. I think you should tell me what this Goon of Fortune game is. Now. *Posted 4hrs ago* [Comment * Like]

> **Tim Hand** It's just like Wheel of Fortune but with a Hill's Hoist, that's all Kim. Completely innocent, nothing to worry about.

Bet no one in Adelaide even knows about it. *Posted 4hrs ago* [Comment * Like]

Katie Black That better be all, Timothy. Jake isn't like the rest of you boys. *Posted 3hrs ago* [Comment * Like]

Jake Black Geez mum, way to be a wet blanket. Just chill. No use bailing Tim up either, he's not my body guard, that's why he's still in Tazzie, dressed in that God-awful jumpsuit, working like the slave he is. I call you, like, every day. Is it so hard to imagine I can manage on my own the rest of the time? *Posted 2hrs ago* [Comment * Like]

Tim Hand You just wait Jakey; by the end of the year you'll wish you were an Elvis impersonator at a Rock & Roll Restaurant rather then one of four hundred engineering students. Not only is it good money, but the chicks dig it. *Posted 2hrs ago* [Comment * Like]

Jake Black The only thing the chicks dig is you finally handing the mic over to Rick, the Buddy Holly Stage Extravaganza. Sorry to step on your blue suede shoes. *Posted 2hrs ago* [Comment * Like]

Katie Black Sorry love, it's only been six months, can you blame a mum for worrying about her son being not home, but a whole ocean away? Love you. *Posted 1hr ago* [Comment * Like]

Jake Black I'll call ya tonight. Next time I'm down we need to set up an FB account for you. Your words next to Katie's name are like looking into a very scary future. *Posted 1hr ago* [Comment * Like]

Katie Black Bite me. *Posted 5mins ago* [Comment * Like]

Jake Black Ah, there she is! *Posted 1min ago* [Comment * Like]

Jake Black has lost his voice. *Posted 02th March 2008 at 14:58* [Comment * Like]

Jake Black 's liver took a beating in college o-week. *Posted 03rd March 2008 at 13:03* [Comment * Like]

> **Amanda Pickup** Go hard or go home Special Boy. *Posted 03rd March 2008 at 13:46* [Comment * Like]
>
> **Jake Black** 'Pickup'? That's not what your name plate says on your door. *Posted 03rd March 2008 at 14:13* [Comment * Like]
>
> **Amanda Pickup** A lady has to let the boys know where she stands these days, they don't pick up hints anymore. *Posted 03rd March 2008 at 14:17* [Comment * Like]
>
> **Jake Black** The K floor boys' rock, I'm sure you'll find one to your liking ? And the walk of shame won't be very far then... *Posted 03rd March 2008 at 14:23* [Comment * Like]
>
> **Amanda Pickup** Just because a girl walks out of another building, dressed in the same clothes as the night before with her heels in her hand and a bit of sex hair, does not mean she should hurry past the dining hall in shame. I will OWN that walk of shame! *Posted 03rd March 2008 at 14:35* [Comment * Like]

Jake Black is 19. *Posted 05nd March 2008 at 09:30* [Comment * Like]

Heather Yosmit Happy b'day. Have an awesome one! See you around, hope you avoid the pond! *Posted 05th March 2008 at 10:20* [Comment * Like]

> **Jake Black** What?? I've been wet for like a week; tell me you only get ponded in o-week? *Posted 05th March 2008 at 11:05* [Comment * Like]

Tim Hand Dude WTF is a ponding? P.S. Happy Birthday, Buddy. *Posted 05th March 2008 at 11:13* [Comment * Like]

Courtney Gimp A ponding ,oh innocent friend of Jake's, is when one picks up the birthday boy or girl and dumps their arse in the courtyard pond. And if they don't put up a good fight we may do it more than once. In regards to what Heather said Jake, you WILL NOT avoid the pond. Put up a good fight kiddo. *Posted 05th March 2008 at 12:00* [Comment * Like]

Kyle Vanders Hey champ, happy b'day... I shall see you at b-ball where we WILL win! Have a top day!! *Posted 05th March 2008 at 15:21* [Comment * Like]

Jasmine Cain Things you should do today; 1. Eat something delicious and fatty. 2. Win basketball. 3. GET SMASHED!!!! *Posted 05th March 2008 at 16:48* [Comment * Like]

Katie Black Happy birthday!!! Welcome 2 ur last yr as a teenager. Enjoy the last yr that u can justify the risk-taking & irresponsible behaviour. Have a gr8 birthday swim, bro! *Posted 05th March 2008 at 17:53* [Comment * Like]

> **Jake Black** First things first: you know how to spell, stop writing like a twelve year old with a pea for a brain. Secondly, thanks. Thirdly... So very, very wet. *Posted 05th March 2008 at 20:20* [Comment * Like]

Jake and **Courtney Gimp** joined the groups **Jagga Bomb Appreciation Society** and **Enjoy it now, because after college it's called alcoholism.** [Join this group]

Kyle Vanders Whoop, whoop! WINNERS!!!!! *Posted 06th March 2008 at 10:11* [Comment * Like]

> **Jake Black** Hypothetical high 5! *Posted 06th March 2008 at 12:19* [Comment * Like]

Jake Black is comfortably numb aka smashed. *Posted 06th March 2008 at 20:36* [Comment * Like]

Jake Black is very seedy. *Posted 07th March 2008 at 19:02* [Comment * Like]

> **Katie Black** Darling, I really hope you are checking your blood sugar levels… *Posted 07th March 2008 at 21:14* [Comment * Like]

> **Jake Black** Mum, seriously! Get off Katie's account! I can take care of myself. *Posted 07th March 2008 at 21:23* [Comment * Like]

> **Katie Black** I know love, I know. But it has only been 6 months and when you're drinking you've got to be careful. *Posted 07th March 2008 at 21:24* [Comment * Like]

> **Jake Black** Stop worrying. Yes it's been six months, *seven* even. I've pricked enough blood to fill a tea cup. I'm fine. How about a happy birthday? *Posted 07th March 2008 at 21:30* [Comment * Like]

> **Katie Black** Happy birthday, love. *Posted 07th March 2008 at 21:31* [Comment * Like]

Jake is attending **Australia's Biggest Morning Tea: College.**

Tim Hand We should probably date. *Posted 28th March 2008 at 19:57* [Comment * Like]

> **Jake Black** What do you mean 'we'? *Posted 29th March 2008 at 12:24* [Comment * Like]

> **Tim Hand** With women you retard. *Posted 29th March 2008 at 22:30* [Comment * Like]

Jake Black is shitttttt bored. *Posted 15th April 2008 at 14:40* [Comment * Like]

Jake now be usin' Ye Olde Facebook in **English (Pirate).**

Cap'n Jake Black Hell yeah, boredom averted. *15th April 'bout 7 shots of rum ago.* [Arrr! * Weigh in]

Th' infamous landlubber Cap'n Jake now be mateys wit **Don Hargrave** n' **3 other pirates.** *3 turns of the hourglass ago.*

Cap'n Jake Black is guitar heroing it up. *10 turn o' the hour glass ago* [Arr! * Weigh In].

Cap'n Jake be admirin' **I don't care how comfortable crocs are, you look like a dumbass** and **There's a good chance I'm an alcoholic, but meh, so are all my friends** an' **5 more scrolls.** *21 shots of rum ago* [Arr! * Weigh In * Fancy th' Anchor]

    Jack Fox an' **8 scallywags** be enjoyin' this.

Jake is now using Facebook in English (UK).

Jake Black is just happy to have survived term 1. Get pumped for pub night! *Posted 23rd April 2008 at 17:37* [Comment * Like]

Jake is attending **Battle of the Bands.**

Jake Black No Mr. Officer, I'm not drunk… I'm just trying to walk like Jack Sparrow. *Posted 23rd April 2008 at 23:54* [Comment * Like]

Jake Black Upon arriving home at 5am discovers he has no door handle. WTF??? *Posted 24th April 2008 at 07:11* [Comment * Like]

Jake Black has a broken jaw. It hurts. *Posted 10th May 2008 at 08:55* [Comment * Like]

    Andy Lambert How did you break your jaw? Lol. *Posted 10th May 2008 at 14:10* [Comment * Like]

    Jake Black WTF! 'A' on Facebook?? *Posted 10th May 2008 at 14:29* [Comment * Like]

Andy Lambert Actually, I got attacked by some people and forced to get Facebook. So here I am... woohoo! Diabetics unite! *Posted 10th May 2008 at 16:36* [Comment * Like]

Jack Black Wicked sick. *Posted 10th May 2008 at 16:44* [Comment * Like]

Amanda Pickup You know, trying out your usual dance moves on skates wasn't the best idea. *Posted 10th May 2008 at 17:09* [Comment * Like]

Jake Black In hindsight skating while seedy, not my best moment. *Posted 10th May 2008 at 17:28* [Comment * Like]

Tim Hand I thought you were going to say something exciting like you got punched in the face. Haha. Well, hope you have a speedy recovery. Yum, soft foods and liquids! Bet you're loving that. *Posted 10th May 2008 at 20:18* [Comment * Like]

Jake Black Bite me. *Posted 10th May 2008 at 21:00* [Comment * Like]

Heather Yosmit Things could have been worse... you could have sliced off limbs with the blade of your skates... *Posted 10th May 2008 at 21:30* [Comment * Like]

Jake Black Instead I can only eat steak that's been through a blender. *Posted 11th May 2008 at 02:40* [Comment * Like]

Jake and **Jasmine Cain** like **Atheist, Agnostic and Non-Religious** and **The official rules of shotgun.** [Like this page]

Andy Lambert Coming to Aust biggest MT? *Posted 30th May 2008 at 09:15* [Comment * Like]

Jake Black Totally. I baked muffins and everything. *Posted 30th May 2008 at 09:20* [Comment * Like]

Andy Lambert What? You're kidding, right? *Posted 30th May 2008 at 09:23* [Comment * Like]

Jake Black No, I'm serious. The chicks dig that shit. *Posted 30th May 2008 at 09:27* [Comment * Like]

Andy Lambert Sure Jakey, blame it on the chicks. Unless you made muffins out of beer, you have just dropped from 'awesome' to 'a little sad' on my cool-o-metre. *Posted 30th May 2008 at 09:34* [Comment * Like]

Jake Black And I'm not at 'pathetic' because? *Posted 30th May 2008 at 09:39* [Comment * Like]

Andy Lambert We shoot-up together. It redeems you, slightly. *Posted 30th May 2008 at 09:42* [Comment * Like]

Jake Black It would sound more bad ass if it wasn't insulin, hey? *Posted 30th May 2008 at 09:50* [Comment * Like]

Andy Lambert Diabetics go harder! *Posted 30th May 2008 at 10:13* [Comment * Like]

Jake Black is studying. *Posted 11th June 2008 at 22:10* [Comment * Like]

Jake Black is procrastinating. *Posted 11th June 2008 at 22:48* [Comment * Like]

Tim Hand While you're procrastinating, I'm overseas tomorrow!! NZ here I come!! *Posted 19th June 2008 at 11:45* [Comment * Like]

Jake Black Hope your ski rebounds off a rock and flicks you in the nuts. *Posted 19th June 2008 at 11:49* [Comment * Like]

Tim Hand No need to be like that, Jakey. We can't all be stuck in the books like you. *Posted 19th June 2008 at 19:21* [Comment * Like]

Jake Black is bored. *Posted 24th June 2008 at 17:13* [Comment * Like]

Jake and **Don Hargrave** like **Mr Squiggle** and **Flight of the Concords** [Like this page]

Jake Black is 4 and a half hours away from freedom/intoxication. *Posted 30th June 2008 at 09:30* [Comment * Like]

Jake Black 4 hours... *Posted 30th June 2008 at 10:00* [Comment * Like]

Jake joined the group **Next semester I'm going to study from the beginning...** [Join group]

Jake Black is getting intoxicated. *Posted 30th June 2008 at 18:54* [Comment * Like]

Don Hargrave Home, sweet home? *Posted 30th June 2008 at 19:31* [Comment * Like]

> **Jake Black** Not yet, got a sup exam in two weeks. *Posted 30th June 2008 at 19:50* [Comment * Like]

> **Don Hargrave** WTF why did you get a sup? *Posted 30th June 2008 at 20:01* [Comment * Like]

> **Jake Black** Diabetes is good for something. Particularly when you want more time to study and drink! *Posted 30th June 2008 at 20:12* [Comment * Like]

> **Don Hargrave** Charlatan. *Posted 30th June 2008 at 20:15* [Comment * Like]

Jake Black is seedy. *Posted 01st July 2008 at 04:18* [Comment * Like]

Jack Black is still seedy. *Posted 01st July 2008 at 06:51* [Comment * Like]

Kyle Vanders Yo, Jakey you missed breakfast. Went hard did ya mate? *Posted 01st July 2008 at 11:20* [Comment * Like]

Andy Lambert Dude you're 20 mins late. Five more mins then I'm busting the door on your arse. I don't care if you're naked! *Posted 01ˢᵗ July 2008 at 13:21* [Comment * Like]

Jake was tagged in **Casey Villa's** photo album **Bitter Sweet Symphony.**

Now what have you done?   [New Message]

[Back to messages * Delete]

Between **Katie Black** and **You.**

Katie Black *01ˢᵗ July 2008 at 17:56* [Report]

Dickhead! You said you would look after yourself! You said you'd be careful! When you get out of your coma I'm going to wring your neck for scaring the shit out of me!

Katie Black *03ʳᵈ July 2008 at 18:19* [Report]

You didn't move. I sang to you for hours and you didn't move. Come back Jakey. Please.

Katie Black *05ᵗʰ July 2008 at 19:32* [Report]

Love you forever.

Heather Yosmit Rest peacefully mate. *Posted 06ᵗʰ July 2008 at 10:08* [Comment * Like]

Amanda Pickup Miss you terribly Jake...Will never forget your whacky dancing or our guitar hero sessions... You were special to all of us at college, we're going to miss you so, so much. No one will ever replace you. *Posted 06th July 2008 at 15:19* [Comment * Like]

Tim Hand Jakey... *Posted 06th July 2008 at 22:15* [Comment * Like]

> **Tim Hand** Sorry mate, I have only just started to believe it and plucked up the courage to write this message on your wall. I'm still overseas and I had to find out through Facebook. God, that hurt. You were always there to brighten the day and see the funny side of everything. Wish we could turn back that clock, eh? Hope you were ripping it up in Adelaide cause I haven't seen you since you left, man. See you in the next life buddy. *Posted 07th July 2008 at 13:22* [Comment * Like]

Kyle Vanders I don't know what to say. You always had so much energy and a crazy appetite for high 5's. Your last name always made me laugh because you were white as an albino and had hair a blond could be proud of. You were pretty much the only person I would stop and talk to on the way to uni, because you always had some epic story to share. College will never be the same without you bud. *Posted 07th July 2008 at 15:52* [Comment * Like]

Andy Lambert Mate, I really miss you. I think of you every day. I wish I could have done more, thought to check sooner, and I'm so sorry you're gone. I'll remember you always; you were one in a million. There is a memorial service this Friday, I will be there for sure. Your diabetic buddy, Andy... Don't forget 'diabetics go harder', miss you mate. *Posted 08th July 2008 at 03:12* [Comment * Like]

Courtney Gimp Miss you dude. Every time I think of you I remember you teaching me how to play the bagpipes in our pre-college days. We were bad, but that was good J xoxo *Posted 08th July 2008 at 11:17* [Comment * Like]

Andy Lambert Had a great year mate. Still missing you and wishing you were here. Finished exams. Uni is as annoying as it always was, and college is just as fun as it always seems to be. Really wish you were here mate, miss you so much. *Posted 22nd November 2008 at 14:53* [Comment * Like]

Katie Black Love you, bro. You are an idiot...were an idiot. But I miss you so much. Always will. *Posted 05th July 2009 at 09:00* [Comment * Like]

Amanda Pickup I got my belly button pierced today ? I remember telling you when we were playing guitar hero how shit scared I was and how I didn't think I'd ever have the courage. But I did it, and it fricken hurt! You told me you thought I was brave to even consider it because there was no way in hell you would. Personally I think you... [See more] *Posted 06th July2009 at 17:42* [Comment * Like]

Don Hargrave Hey buddy, happy 21st birthday! I had a few (15 or so) drinks for you, no doubt you are getting your drink on by now. Remember the time you and I cleared the d-floor in 3secs due to our ridiculous dance moves? Everyone thought we were idiots. I thought we were pretty cool. Whenever I see someone dancing their heart out, they remind me of you. *Posted 05th March 2010 at 10:57* [Comment * Like]

Tim Hand Happy birthday old boy ? Got your initials tattooed on me a few weeks back. Always missing you man, can't believe it's nearly 3 years. Love Tim xx *Posted 05th March 2010 at 16:33* [Comment * Like]

Andy Lambert Hey mate, haven't been on Facebook much lately, seems I missed your b'day by a long shot. I'm having a drink for you. Just been taking this semester off, taking it easy. Not at college anymore, had enough of all that last year and moved out. Try to keep up with people. Still have nightmares. And I still miss you, mate. *Posted 23rd March 2010 at 15:15* [Comment * Like]

Jake's Page: A Play

First Performed By

Urban Myth Youth Theatre

Adelaide, SA

June 2012

Jake's Page: A Play – Small Cast

CHARACTERS

JAKE BLACK: 19 year old university student, just moved into college, type 1 diabetic. Basketball fanatic, high fiver, habit of dancing like a crazy person.

TIM HAND: Jake's best friend from high school lives in Tasmania.

KATIE BLACK: 16 year old sister of Jake.

AMANDA PICKUP: Friend of Jake.

ANDY LAMBERT: Friend of Jake, type 1 diabetic.

COURNEY GIMP: Older collegian female.

KYLE VANDERS: Older collegian male.

FACEBOOK: Embodiment of Facebook, dressed in white. They always speak in an overly enthusiastic voice.

SCENE:

Down stage is a small desk and chair facing the audience, a bed and door/ door frame at the back of the stage behind the desk. Jake's scenes occur in this space. Arrayed in a semi-circle around Jake are 6 black boxes where the characters stand. All characters interacting with Jake have an assigned box in this circle. Facebook roams between them and jumps about as they say their lines.

FACEBOOK: *[Overly enthusiastic]* Add Jake Black as a friend! Jake is studying Mechanical Engineering at Uni of Adelaide. Jake lives in Adelaide, South Australia, but is from Hobart! Born 5th of March 1989.

> *[As the curtain rises* JAKE, *white skinned, blond hair, walks into his room with suitcase in tow and starts to set up. First thing he does is place his laptop on the desk and open it, he sits down facing the audience and types for several seconds.]*

FACEBOOK: Jake and Tim are now friends. Jake joined the group Melbourne is a backwater, but Adelaide's a city with balls! *[Starts pleading/questioning the audience]* Want to join the group? Come on, do it! Join us. It's a great group.

> *[JAKE continues to set up his room.* TIM, *is lounging in a chair with a video game controller in his hand. He plays animatedly as he speaks.]*

FACEBOOK: Tim Hand updated his status!

TIM HAND: Dear Facebook, just wait, one day they'll abandon you as well, Sincerely MySpace… Why are we here again? What's wrong with Myspace?

JAKE BLACK: We are here because you decided to stay behind on the Island of the devil while I party it up at uni. Also, Facebook is the bomb!!!!!

TIM HAND: No, I'm the bomb, Facebook is the devil.

JAKE BLACK: Don't be such a grandpa!!!!

TIM HAND: Fine. I'll stay on Facebook, but only if you take a minimalist approach to exclamation marks

JAKE BLACK: Done.

> *[TIM leaves and KATIE comes on holding a mirror, preening*

and putting on lip stick. JAKE *is holding a bed sheet and attempts to create a toga from it as Katie speaks. He takes periodic swigs from a beer bottle on his desk.]*

FACEBOOK: Katie Black PM'd you!

KATIE BLACK: Let's face it; I couldn't wait to see the back of your face. But then you didn't turn around and wave to me when you went through the gate. Which is completely unfair! I'm the nice one in this brother-sister relationship; you should have been bawling your eyes out while I merrily kicked you on the plane. Way to ruin the fantasy.

[Music blares loudly. JAKE's *toga efforts are hampered by his unusual and erratic dancing.* KYLE *knocks hard on Jake's door as Jake tries to fix on the toga with an ineffective knot.]*

KYLE VANDERS: It's time Fresher Fuck!

JAKE BLACK: *[Turns and does some hasty typing]* Just stay out of trouble drama queen. Miss your face. *[Opens door]*

KATIE BLACK: You're impossible.

KYLE VANDERS: Too late! On your knees! *[Holds up a goon bag and pours directly into Jake's mouth for several seconds. Gives Jake a slap on the back]* Right, forward march! Dance boy! Dance!

*[*JAKE *dances off stage with* KYLE. *Possible Facebook Ad's assault Katie eg. 'Buy a goldfish!', 'dresses for cats!' etc]*

FACEBOOK: *[Hovers near Katie]* Katie Black joined the group 'I'm the only normal one in my family'. *[Pauses as though processing distant information]* Status Update from Kyle Vanders! Man this fresher must be allergic to beer because he's dancing like a puppet on magic mushrooms.

COURTNEY GIMP: With party skills like that there's only one nickname for him… Special Boy!

FACEBOOK: Status Update from Kyle Vanders! Bahahaha, Jake just fell into the Torrens! Funniest thing I've seen this o-week.

> [*At the end of the Ad sequence* JAKE, ANDY *and* KYLE *stumble back into Jake's room, beer in hand, arms around each other, singing drunkenly. The toga is now soaking wet and draped around Jake's neck. They deposit their bottles on the desk, which continues to grow during the act. Jake misses a high 5 with Andy several times before connecting. Andy stumbles away. Jake collapses on bed with the help of Kyle.*]

KYLE VANDERS: You're alright mate, you're alright. [*Removes the toga and Jake's shoes. He leans in close, and speaks in a whisper*] Don't forget to have a little shoot up before you go to bed, ok?

> [*Jake nods, Kyle returns to his box. Jake stumbles to the desk and rummages through a draw, pulling out a small black bag. He faces his back to the audience for several seconds. When he turns around he holds a needle in one hand. He stabs it into his stomach, throws the needle on the desk then collapses on his bed.*]

> [TIM *moves his chair to sit closer to Jake's bed; he has a computer in his lap. Jake continues to lie asleep. Between them is* FACEBOOK.]

FACEBOOK: [*In a overly happy voice*] Tim Hand poked you. [*Pokes Jake*]

> [*Jake shrieks and sits up rubbing his eyes, Tim sniggers*]

FACEBOOK: Tim Hand threw a cow at you [*Shoves a stuffed toy at Jake bowling him off the bed. Jake staggers back up*] Tim Hand stuffed ice-cream down your pants [*goes to pull out the front of Jake's pants, Jake slaps* *him away. Facebook pauses.]* You wish to slap Tim? *[Jake nods. Facebook turns and slaps Tim across the face]* Your slap has been sent.

[Jake collapses back onto the bed only to have his door burst open. Jake is rushed off stage by several people then returned to down stage dressed in lederhosen and a goon box strapped to his head. AMANDA next to him is wearing a bathing suit with green plastic leaves stuck over the breasts and pelvic area, Adam and Eve style. A series of Tableaus follow, in each Tableau Jake and Amanda move closer together. In first Tableau Jake and Amanda are reacting to each other's costumes]

FACEBOOK: Kyle Vanders posted a photo in the album 'O-week Drop-Offs'.

TIM HAND: Dude! WTF. Where are you??

JAKE BLACK: Ok, first of all, I want to say I did NOT dress myself like this. I was ambushed. Seriously mate, would I be wearing THIS if I was lying? According to the college rule book it was expected. I mean, it's definitely expected that your locked door will open at 6am and you'll be held down while some senior collegian uses you as a canvas. It's perfectly normal right?

FACEBOOK: Kyle Vanders marked this photo's location as Handorf, local German Town.

[Amanda and Jake move into another tableau. Two more people join them. One looks confused and leans in as though to poke Jake's pants, the other stares at his crotch]

FACEBOOK: Courney Gimp posted a photo of you with the caption-

COURTNEY GIMP: The Freshers finally meet the locals.

FACEBOOK: Like!

AMANDA PICKUP: OMG. You posted my most embarrassing moment on Facebook!

JAKE BLACK: You've got to give Duncan credit, it took most people ages to realise the lederhosen was painted on and not real clothing.

> *[The person who was poking leaps back in horror. The person staring at the crotch takes a step forward for a closer look. Freeze in new position]*

I think the buckles super glued to my nipples were the main perpetrator of *that* illusion.

FACEBOOK: Like!

KATIE BLACK: Bro, the look that woman is giving you could peel paint!

KYLE VANDERS: You in time will learn this look, Sister of Jake. Where the parents judge you as the drunken deviant you are and young girls, like yourself, try to take a closer look at your junk.

KATIE BLACK: EEEWWWWW!

JAKE BLACK: *[grins madly]* It was awesome!

KATIE BLACK: Well you're deranged!

> *[New Tableau, Jake and Amanda realise they have no wallet or phone]*

FACEBOOK: Kyle Vanders posted a new photo captioned-

KYLE VANDERS: When they finally realised they had no phone or wallet to get back to Adelaide.

AMANDA PICKUP: Kyle you are a lunatic! You realise this, right?

FACEBOOK: Jake Black likes Amanda's comment!

JAKE BLACK: Yes... trying to get back without money is not quite as awesome as scaring off young children.

AMANDA PICKUP: Try hitch-hiking when you are with someone who looks like he paints himself rather than buying pants.

[Tableau changes to Jake and Amanda trying to hitchhike]

TIM HAND: Comment! Dude is that a *Goon box* on your head? No wonder the oldies thought you were drunk! Were you playing that Goon of Fortune game I've been hearing about?

JAKE BLACK: Comment! So *that's* why they kept driving past!

COURTNEY GIMP: Comment! Or because they thought you were spreading the word of the Lord.

KYLE VANDERS: Comment! Or because you looked like part of a travelling circus.

TIM HAND: Comment! Or because you looked like you were mugged at a yodelling competition.

AMANDA PICKUP: Comment! Either way it didn't work!

[Change tableau to Jake and Amanda trying to catch a bus. A DRIVER looks at them with an expression on the tipping point of extreme horror and hysterical laughter]

FACEBOOK: Kyle Vanders posted a photo captioned-

KYLE VANDERS: Please explain.

COURTNEY GIMP: Comment! That driver's response was a crack up! *[puts on a mocking voice]* "You expect me to believe, that around 50 teenagers are dressed like this every year and dropped off all around Adelaide, without a single fight to keep your clothes on? Without a single hidden dollar up the who-ha?" *[normal voice]* Classic!

FACEBOOK: Comment! LOL.

KYLE VANDERS: *[Kyle Vanders starts laughing really hard, and has to calm himself down to speak]* Then he said, "If I see you out here again in anything less than snow gear, I'm going to run you over with this bus."

FACEBOOK: Jake Black updated his status!

JAKE BLACK: Does anyone have a good method for removing superglue from skin? *[Points to buckles stuck to nipples]*

[Jake returns to his room, puts a shirt and pants on over his lederhosen. Has a couple of beers with ANDY and KYLE.]

JAKE BLACK: My blood is now 100% beer. So long o-week, and thanks for all the fish!

[Collapses on bed, Andy and Kyle return to their boxes. AMANDA appears dressed in jogging gear and stretching.]

JAKE BLACK: Jake's liver took a beating in college o-week.

AMANDA PICKUP: You want to be a real boy? Go hard or go home Special Boy.

JAKE BLACK: *[Slight groan in voice over as though hung-over]* You're seriously going with Amanda Pickup for your Facebook profile? That's not what your name plate says on your door.

AMANDA PICKUP: A lady has to let the boys know where she stands these days; they don't pick up hints anymore.

[Facebook converges on Jake circling him.]

FACEBOOK: Andy Lambert ploughed your field!

[Jake frowns]

FACEBOOK: Courtney Gimp stewed your apples! Kyle Vanders milked your cows! *[Chant]* Play FarmVille. Play Farmville. Play Farmville. Play Farmville. Play Farmville.

[Jake screams and flaps the offending Farmville demon away.]

JAKE BLACK: Where were we?

FACEBOOK: A lady has to let the boys know where she stands these days; they don't pick up hints

JAKE BLACK: Aha! Us college boys' are pretty awesome, I'm sure you'll find one to your liking. And the walk of shame won't be very far then...

AMANDA PICKUP: *[Tartly]* Just because a girl walks out of college building, dressed in the same clothes as the night before, with her heels in her hand and a bit of sex hair, does not mean she should hurry past the dining hall in shame. I will OWN that walk of shame!

[As Amanda goes to stride past Jake's door, Jake manages to get off his bed, open his door a crack and watch her go past. Amanda stands on her box again.]

FACEBOOK: Kyle Vanders just updated his-

KYLE VANDERS: *[Interjects]* ooohhhhh! Jakey's perving on Amanda!

[Jake makes a rude gesture at Kyle, goes into his room, sits at his desk and sighs.]

FACEBOOK: Jake Black updated his status.

JAKE BLACK: is BBBOOOOORRREEEDDDD

[Jake tinkers on the computer for a minute. A murmuring starts in the background. As it gets louder you can make out the

words '21 shots of rum'. This continues at a moderate volume. FACEBOOK jumps out with a pirate patch over one eye.]

FACEBOOK: Arrrr! Jake now be usin' Ye Olde Facebook in Pirate English.

JAKE BLACK: Hell yeah, boredom averted! *[Sits back to watch the action]*

FACEBOOK: Th' infamous landlubber Cap'n Jake now be mateys wit Kyle Vanders n' three other pirates.

ALL: *[uproariously]* 21 shots of rum ago!

FACEBOOK: Cap'n Jake be admirin' 'I don't care how comfortable crocs are, you look like a dumbass' an' 5 more scrolls.

GROUP 1: Arr!

GROUP 2: Weigh in!

GROUP 3: Fancy th' Anchor!

FACEBOOK: Cap'n Courtney gimp an' 8 scallywags be enjoyin' this.

ALL: 21 shots of rum ago!

FACEBOOK: Cap'n Jake an' Cap'n Tim Hand be admirin' 'Jagga Bomb Appreciation Society' an' 'The Drunken Text Appreciation Society'

ALL: 21 shots of rum ago!

GROUP 2: Arr!

GROUP 3: Weigh In!

GROUP 1: Fancy th' Anchor!

FACEBOOK: Cap'n Jake an' Cap'n Courtney joined the ship, 'Enjoy it now, because after college it's called alcoholism'.

ALL: Arr! Crew th' ship ye scallywags!

FACEBOOK: Cap'n Jake be buryin' treasure at 'Battle of th' Bands'. Cap'n Jake an' Cap'n Katie Black be admirin' 'The official rules of shotgun'.

ALL: 21 shots of rum ago!

GROUP 3: Arr!

GROUP 1: Weight In!

GROUP 2: Fancy th' Anchor!

FACEBOOK: *[Cuts in on the fun]* Jake Black is now using Facebook in English, UK.

> *[Facebook sighs and steps back. Jake cracks open a beer and sits at his desk.]*

JAKE BLACK: Has lost his voice. And is 20.

AMANDA PICKUP: Happy b'day. Have an awesome one! See you around, hope you avoid the pond!

JAKE BLACK: *[Jake spurts beer to one side]* What?? I've been wet for like a week; tell me you only get ponded in o-week?

> *[Amanda stands there grinning.]*

TIM HAND: Dude what the fuck is a ponding? P.S. Happy Birthday, Buddy.

COURTNEY GIMP: A ponding, oh innocent friend of Jake's, is when one picks up the birthday boy or girl and dumps their arse in the courtyard pond.

[KYLE and ANDY enter and knock hard on Jake's door. Jake stares at it in comic horror. As Courtney continues to speak, Jake holds onto the door to try and stop the boys from getting in, but is unsuccessful. A struggle ensures]

COURTNEY GIMP: And if they don't put up a good fight we may do it more than once. In regards to what Amanda said Jake, you WILL NOT avoid the pond. Put up a good fight kiddo.

[JAKE gets carried out of his room. KYLE re-enters stage, moves onto his box, without Jake. Jake makes his way back to his room, hair damp, clothes wet. He glares at the computer as Kyle speaks]

Kyle Vanders Hey champ, happy b'day… Nice swim? The best start to a top day! I shall see you at b-ball where we WILL win! *[Spins an imaginary ball on his finger]*

[Rest of actors are happily creating a chatting background hum. Jake starts to get ready for Basketball, towelling his hair dry etc]

KATIE BLACK: Happy birthday!!! Welcome 2 ur last yr as a teenager. Enjoy the last yr that u can justify the risk-taking & irresponsible behaviour. Have a gr8 birthday swim, bro!

JAKE BLACK: *[Jake pauses to type]* First things first: you know how to spell, stop writing like a twelve year old with a pea for a brain. Secondly, thanks. Thirdly… So very, very wet.

[Jake pauses, starting at the desk drawer. He shrugs, opens it and pulls out the little black bag. He turns his back to the audience again. Shaking a hand, he turns around sucking his finger, he pulls out a needle, sticks it into his stomach. He cracks his neck, has jump to shake himself out and leaves the room. KYLE stays on box]

KYLE VANDERS: Whoop, whoop! WINNERS!!!!! *[Mimes lining up a ball and scoring]*

JAKE BLACK: *[Still off stage]* Hypothetical high 5!

[JAKE comes into his room with another drink, and collapses happily in his chair.]

JAKE BLACK: No Mr. Officer, I'm not drunk... I'm just trying to walk like Jack Sparrow. *[In a dream, he reaches into the black bag and uses another needle. Types again.]* Jake is comfortably numb aka smashed. *[Jake appears to sleep in the chair.]*

FACEBOOK: Amanda Pickup posted an update.

AMANDA PICKUP: It's 4am and my door knobs missing. WTF!

FACEBOOK: Courtney Gimp updated her status.

COURTNEY GIMP: 5 am and only 2 hours and 1000words until this baby needs to be handed in. Come on Red Bull, give me wings!

[Jake opens his eyes and types one fingered.]

FACEBOOK: Jake Black is very seedy.

[KATIE, standing tall and wearing 'grandma clothes', speaks in a 'grown up' voice]

KATIE BLACK: Darling, I really hope you are taking care of yourself. With your condition you have to be careful.

[Jake looks confused. Then his face clears.]

JAKE BLACK: Mum, seriously! Get off Katie's account! I can take care of myself.

KATIE BLACK: I know love, I know. But it has only been 6 months and when you're drinking you've got to really watch out.

JAKE BLACK: Stop worrying. I've pricked enough blood to fill a tea cup. I'm fine. How about a happy birthday?

KATIE BLACK: Happy birthday, love.

JAKE BLACK: Next time I'm home we need to set up an FB account for you. Your words next to Katie's name are like looking into a very scary future.

KATIE BLACK: *[Normal voice]* Bite me.

> *[AMANDA walks on dressed only in a towel with cupcakes on it. She pauses in Jake's doorway.]*

AMANDA PICKUP: Hey Jake, going to Australia's Biggest morning Tea?

> *[Jake turns and freezes, hand raised in an idiotic wave. He manages to nod]*

AMANDA PICKUP: Sweet, can't wait to see what you make. *[Waves and sallies off stage]*

> *[Jake turns back to computer. FACEBOOK jumps forward enthusiastically]*

FACEBOOK: Jake is attending Australia's Biggest Morning Tea: College.

ANDY LAMBERT: Coming to Aust biggest MT?

JAKE BLACK: WTF! A on Facebook??

ANDY LAMBERT: Actually, I got attacked by some people and forced to get Facebook. So here I am... woohoo! *[He picks up the black bag from in front of him and pulls out a needle like Jake's. He lifts up the edge of his shorts and sticks it into his thigh.]*

JAKE BLACK: Wicked sick.

ANDY LAMBERT: Getting high on life baby. *[Andy throws needle back into the back.]* So are you coming?

JAKE BLACK: Totally. I baked muffins and everything.

ANDY LAMBERT: What? You're kidding, right?

JAKE BLACK: No, I'm serious. The chicks dig that shit. And I'm a chick magnet, enough said. Have to beat them off with a stick.

[Jake watches the door. He jumps up as AMANDA walks past again and he waves a little too eagerly.]

ANDY LAMBERT: Sure Jakey, blame it on the chicks. Unless you made muffins out of beer, you have just dropped from 'awesome' to 'a little sad' on my cool-o-metre.

JAKE BLACK: And I'm not at 'pathetic' because?

ANDY LAMBERT: We shoot-up together. It redeems you, slightly.

[They both grin and look at their black bags]

JAKE BLACK: It would sound more bad ass if it wasn't insulin, hey?

ANDY LAMBERT: Diabetics go harder!

[Jake lies down on his bed]

FACEBOOK: Status update from Courtney Gimp.

COURTNEY GIMP: It's official. Special Boy has broken the Jagga Bomb record, 5 in a row!

KYLE VANDERS: Impressed, Jakey managed to play a good game of B-ball after yesterday's Jagga fest.

FACEBOOK: Andy Lambert posted on your wall!

ANDY LAMBERT: Keen for a skate?

[With a groan JAKE sits up and goes to sit at his desk. His nose is heavily strapped with tape. He has a dark ring on one eye. ANDY, TIM, AMANDA crowd around Jake on the bed.]

JAKE BLACK: Jake has a broken nose. It hurts.

ANDY LAMBERT: So you did end up breaking your nose? Lol.

AMANDA PICKUP: You know, trying out your usual dance moves on skates wasn't the best idea.

JAKE BLACK: In hindsight skating while seedy, not my best moment. *[goes to rest his face in his hands and pulls back, wincing]*

TIM HAND: Yum, soft foods and liquids! Bet you're loving that.

JAKE BLACK: Bite me.

AMANDA PICKUP: Things could have been worse... you could have sliced off limbs with the blade of your skates...

[Tim, Amanda and Andy back off to their boxes. Andy whispers to FACEBOOK and hands them an envelope. FACEBOOK knocks on Jake's door.]

FACEBOOK: *[overly cheerful voice]* Personal message from Andy Lambert to Jake Black.

[Jake takes envelope, and sits at his desk with a groan]

ANDY LAMBERT: Hey Jakey. Are you alright? It's just, you've been seedy a lot mate. I mean don't get me wrong, you do some funny shit when you're hung over; the penguin dive across the ice was epic. But you don't have to go as hardcore as the old blokes at college. They don't really give a shit if you drink like a fish or not.

[Jake massages his temples in agitation then taps the keyboard forcefully]

JAKE BLACK: Thanks for your nosy concern, but for your information I was not drunk when we were skating, I had a flipping low blood sugar level. Alright?

ANDY LAMBERT: *[Pause]* Wanna talk about it?

JAKE BLACK: *[Angry]* About what? The fact that I have to watch everything that I eat? That even watching what I eat isn't enough? Because if I get the carb count wrong and take the wrong dose my blood sugar bounces like a yoyo and I feel shit for days? The fact that I have to plan every inch of my day so there is no room left for any sort of spontaneous activity at all?

ANDY LAMBERT: *[comforting]* I know you're new to this, but I can promise you, from someone who has gone through that shitty learning curve, you get used to it.

JAKE BLACK: I don't want to get *used* to it, Andy! Thinking to myself, I shouldn't eat that, I'll get heart disease. Going from playing b-ball every day to only twice a week because I can't be assed checking my sugar levels before, during and after.

ANDY LAMBERT: I hear you; trying to psych yourself up to inject insulin four times a day is bad enough without having to do it three times a game!

JAKE BLACK: I hate being part of this, this *club*. The diabetics club, where every new person you meet puts in their 2 cents about a friend, cousin, grandparent or neighbour who has it, and how the person they know can't do 'this or that', and am I *sure* I'm allow to do that?

TOGETHER: YES I'M BLOODY SURE!!!

JAKE BLACK: I'm not some old fat geezer who got that way because I didn't look after myself! *[Bursts into tears]*

ANDY LAMBERT: *[light-heartedly]* Then there's the whole issue of trying to look manly while carrying a bag everywhere you go, hey? Damn Target never took needles into consideration when they designed their pockets, the bastards.

[Jake shorts with laughter half-way through his sobs]

There's nothing we can't eat or do we just need to think ahead before we do it.

JAKE BLACK: Before, I didn't have to think about it or plan ahead, I just did it. I'm not like you. Then in two days I went from normal to watching everything I eat, and staring at a needle for twenty minutes trying to convince myself I need it to live. If you don't get it right and go low, you could die, if you don't get it right and go high you damage your organs and end up with one of a hundred extra diseases when you get older. So basically, if you don't get the balance right, you're fucked. And as a newbie you *never* get it right, so you're always fucked. When someone suggests something as simple as going out for a drink or dinner after uni, I want to say yes rather than have to say no every time because I don't have the right insulin with me. I just want to be normal Andy, so all I have to worry about is girls and the fact I'm rooted for exams. That's what happens when you choose the wrong course just so you can get away from your parents.

ANDY LAMBERT: There is no such thing as normal mate. So many people would look at college and say, doing that shit and drinking that much isn't normal.

JAKE BLACK: Drinking is something I can control, if I know it's coming and I can just be like every other happy go lucky dickhead out there. Diabetes doesn't *own* me. I plan ahead now, not to avoid dying, but so I can live!

ANDY LAMBERT: When I first found out I had it, I was pissed off at everyone. It took me a good 6 months to realise it wasn't going away and I wasn't helping anyone by being angry, least of all myself. It's a conscious decision you have to make. But don't forget, I'm here for ya mate.

JAKE BLACK: Thanks.

[Jake sighs, and fetches a large pile of papers onto his desk. Starts looking all over his room, bitting his nails, and doing anything other than looking at the papers.]

JAKE BLACK: Is shitttttt bored. *[Pauses for a moment, sighs]* Is studying.

[TIM enters stage, all rugged up with a beanie and scarf]

TIM HAND: While you're procrastinating, I'm overseas tomorrow!! NZ here I come!!

JAKE BLACK: Hope your ski rebounds off a rock and flicks you in the nuts.

TIM HAND: No need to be like that, Jakey. We can't all be stuck in the books like you.

[AMANDA busts into JAKE's room holding two fake guitars]

AMANDA PICKUP: Bored?

JAKE BLACK: Jake is guitar heroing it up!

[Jake and Amanda start to play guitar hero in the room. There is a hum in the background made up by the arrayed characters who are 'on Facebook'. Jake and Amanda collapse in a heap laughing. Jake leans in and kisses her. Amanda and Jake pull apart. Amanda, all coy, points to the papers and then leaves. Jake sits at his desk with a big grin]

FACEBOOK: Comment from Tim Hand!

TIM HAND: We should probably date.

JAKE BLACK: *[startled out of his daydream]* What do you mean 'we'?

TIM HAND: With women you retard.

JAKE BLACK: Owch, way to assume I'm as retarded as you!

TIM HAND: Jake, I've never seen anyone less of a player then you. There's no way you've scored already.

[Tim leaves. Jake plays with paper and becomes more panicky]

JAKE BLACK: Jake is 4 and a half hours away from freedom/ intoxication. *[Riffles through paper frantically]* 4 hours…

[Before Jake rushes out the door he turns and types.]

FACEBOOK: Jake joined the group Next semester I'm going to study from the beginning. *[Starts pointing people out in the crowd]* You should probably join to. Oh, and you. And you, yes you, you definitely look like a slacker. Another Facebook group should do you good.

[Andy and Jake both leave the stage]

FACEBOOK: Status update from Andy Lambert. This exam is going to be awesome thanks to my handy faculty-approved cheat sheet! *[Pauses]* Status update from Jake Black. Holy shit! We were allowed flipping cheat sheets! Why didn't anyone tell me! *[Pauses]* Status update from Andy Lambert. That test was easier then letting rip after some baked beans. *[Pause]* Status update from Jake Black. Answer to Question 4 – Picture of an elephant. Perhaps I'll get sympathy marks for my artistic ability.

[JAKE returns and throws his bag on the bed. He scoops up several beer bottles]

JAKE BLACK: Jake is getting intoxicated.

[Dances out of the room. Several Tableaus of him partying, initially standing up and as the tableaus progress he gets closer and closer to the ground. He returns to his room, stumbling. He drops empty bottles across his desk.]

JAKE BLACK: Is seedy.

[He reaches for his black bag and with much fumbling, manages to prick his finger in view of the audience and press it against a small machine. He picks up a needle from the bag but drops it under the bed. He types]

JAKE BLACK: Is still seedy.

[He lies on the floor and reaches under the bed groping blindly. When he doesn't find it he lets his head drop to the floor and closes his eyes. Jake remains still on his floor.]

KYLE VANDERS: *[Eating from a bowl]* Yo, Jakey you missed breakfast. Went hard did ya mate?

ANDY LAMBERT: Dude you're 20 mins late. 5 more mins then I'm busting the door on your arse. I don't care if you're naked!

[Kyle and Andy march over to Jake's door. After trying the doorknob several times and knocking, Kyle leaves and returns with a set of keys. They unlock the door to find Jake on the ground. They go through the motions of tying to wake him up. Andy rushes to the black bag but finds it empty. They call emergency services and the stage lights on Jake's room go out. FACEBOOK with a white envelope wanders around the stage and Jake's room looking lost. It stands uncertainly in the middle of Jake's room]

FACEBOOK: *[Uncertain and lost]* Personal message for Jake Black from Katie Black. Message subject: Now what have you done?

[A pacing KATIE enters stage left. She is angry.]

KATIE BLACK: Dickhead! You said you would look after yourself! You said you'd be careful! When you get out of your coma I'm going to wring your neck for scaring the shit out of me!

[Katie walks through Jake's door and sits on the bed staring blankly ahead.]

KATIE BLACK: You didn't move. I sang to you for hours and you didn't move. Come back Jakey. Please.

[After staring into space collapses on the floor]

KATIE BLACK: Love you forever.

[Katie leaves stage. TIM, AMANDA, COURTNEY, ANDY and KYLE are arrayed in a semi-circle on stage. Kyle looks crushed, and Andy sits in a ball on the floor gripping his black bag tight. The other three are typing away unconcerned, at their laptops sitting on their knees. Kyle finally takes a deep breath and types]

KYLE VANDERS: Rest peacefully mate.

[Tim, Amanda and Courtney all stiffen, looking at the computer in disbelief]

AMANDA PICKUP: *[Stands up and moves into Jake's room]* Miss you terribly Jake…Will never forget your whacky dancing or our guitar hero sessions… You were special to all of us at college; we're going to miss you so, so much. No one will ever replace you. *[She slowly collapses at the foot of Jake's Bed]*

COURTNEY GIMP: I don't know what to say. You always had so much energy and a crazy appetite for high five's. Your last name always made me laugh because you were white as an albino and had hair a blond could be proud of. You were pretty much the only person I would stop and talk to on the way to uni, because you always had some epic story to share.

TIM HAND: Jakey… *[Pauses, overcome.]* Sorry mate, I have only just started to believe it and plucked up the courage to write this message on your wall. I'm still overseas and I had to find out through Facebook. God, that hurt. You were always there to brighten the day and see the funny side of everything. Wish we could turn back that clock, eh? Hope you were ripping it up in Adelaide cause I haven't seen you since you left, man. See you in the next life buddy.

ANDY LAMBERT: *[In anguish, frequent pauses]* Mate, I really miss you. I think of you every day. I wish I could have done more, thought to check sooner, and I'm so sorry you're gone. I'll remember you always; you were one in a million. There is a memorial service this Friday; I will be there for sure. Your diabetic buddy, Andy… Don't forget 'diabetics go harder', *[whispers]* miss you mate.

[KATIE walks into his room. She closes his laptop, picks up Jake's suitcase and leaves. FACEBOOK enters stage with a white envelope and wanders, lost, as they speak.]

FACEBOOK: Personal Message from Andy Lambert to Jake Black. Message subject: I can't believe it's been a year.

ANDY LAMBERT: Hey mate, haven't been on Facebook much lately. Just been taking this semester off, taking it easy. Not at college anymore, had enough of all that last year and moved out. Try to keep up with people. *[Pauses, serious]* Still have nightmares. And I still miss you, mate.

[Stage to black]

END

Jake's Page: A Play - Large Cast

JAKE BLACK: 19 year old university student, just moved into college, type 1 diabetic. Basketball fanatic, high fiver, habit of dancing like a crazy person. (Assigned to FACEBOOK 1)

TIM HAND: Jake's best friend from high school lives in Tasmania. (Assigned to FACEBOOK 2)

KATIE BLACK: 16 year old sister of Jake. (Assigned to FACEBOOK 3)

AMANDA PICKUP: Friend of Jake. (Assigned to FACEBOOK 4)

ANDY LAMBERT: Friend of Jake, type 1 diabetic. (Assigned to FACEBOOK 5)

COURNEY GIMP: Older collegian female. (Assigned to FACEBOOK 6)

KYLE VANDERS: Older collegian male. (Assigned to FACEBOOK 7)

FACEBOOK 1-FACEBOOK 7 : Embodiments of Facebook, assigned to a character, dressed in white. They always speak in overly enthusiastic voices.

SCENE:

Down stage is a small desk and chair facing the audience, a bed and door/ door frame at the back of the stage behind the desk. Jake's scenes occur in this space. Arrayed in a semi-circle around Jake are 6 black boxes where the characters stand. All characters interacting with Jake have an assigned box in this circle. Their assigned 'Facebookers' (FACEBOOK 1-7) stand beside them. Facebook 1-7 who are 'embodying' Facebook jump out onto stage as they say their lines.

FACEBOOK 7: *[Overly enthusiastic]* Add Jake Black as a friend!

FACEBOOK 6: Jake is studying Mechanical Engineering at Uni of Adelaide.

FACEBOOK 3: Jake lives in Adelaide, South Australia–

FACEBOOK 4: *[butts in]* But is from Hobart!

FACEBOOK 5: Born 5th of March 1989.

> *[As the curtain rises JAKE, white skinned, blond hair, walks into his room with suitcase in tow and starts to set up. First thing he does is place his laptop on the desk and open it, he sits down facing the audience and types for several seconds.]*

FACEBOOK 2: Jake and Tim are now friends.

FACEBOOK 1: Jake joined the group Melbourne is a backwater, but Adelaide's a city with balls! *[Starts pleading/questioning the audience]* Want to join the group? Come on, do it! Join us. It's a great group.

> *[JAKE continues to set up his room. TIM, is lounging in a chair with a video game controller in his hand. He plays animatedly as he speaks.]*

FACEBOOK 2: Tim Hand updated his status!

TIM HAND: Dear Facebook, just wait, one day they'll abandon you as well, Sincerely MySpace… Why are we here again? What's wrong with Myspace?

FACEBOOK 1: Comment! From Jake Black.

JAKE BLACK: We are here because you decided to stay behind on the Island of the devil while I party it up at uni. Also, Facebook is the bomb!!!!!

TIM HAND: No, I'm the bomb, Facebook is the devil.

JAKE BLACK: Don't be such a grandpa!!!!

TIM HAND: Fine. I'll stay on Facebook, but only if you take a minimalist approach to exclamation marks

JAKE BLACK: Done.

> *[TIM leaves and KATIE comes on holding a mirror, preening and putting on lip stick. JAKE is holding a bed sheet and attempts to create a toga from it as Katie speaks. He takes periodic swigs from a beer bottle on his desk.]*

FACEBOOK 3: Katie Black PM'd you!

KATIE BLACK: Let's face it; I couldn't wait to see the back of your face. But then you didn't turn around and wave to me when you went through the gate. Which is completely unfair! I'm the nice one in this brother-sister relationship; you should have been bawling your eyes out while I merrily kicked you on the plane. Way to ruin the fantasy.

> *[Music blares loudly. JAKE's toga efforts are hampered by his unusual and erratic dancing. KYLE knocks hard on Jake's door as Jake tries to fix on the toga with an ineffective knot.]*

KYLE VANDERS: It's time Fresher Fuck!

JAKE BLACK: *[Turns and does some hasty typing]* Just stay out of trouble drama queen. Miss your face. *[Opens door]*

KATIE BLACK: You're impossible.

KYLE VANDERS: Too late! On your knees! *[Holds up a goon bag and pours directly into Jake's mouth for several seconds. Gives Jake a slap on the back]* Right, forward march! Dance boy! Dance!

> *[JAKE danced off stage with KYLE.   Possible Facebook Ad's assault Katie]*

FACEBOOK 3: Katie Black joined the group 'I'm the only normal one in my family'.

FACEBOOK 7: Status Update from Kyle Vanders! Man this fresher must be allergic to beer because he's dancing like a puppet on magic mushrooms.

FACEBOOK 6: Comment from Courtney Gimp!

COURTNEY GIMP: With party skills like that there's only one nickname for him... Special Boy!

FACEBOOK 7: Status Update from Kyle Vanders! Bahahaha, Jake just fell into the Torrens! Funniest thing I've seen this o-week.

> *[At the end of the Ad sequence JAKE, ANDY and KYLE stumble back into Jake's room, beer in hand, arms around each other, singing drunkenly. The toga is now soaking wet and draped around Jake's neck. They deposit their bottles on the desk, which continues to grow during the act. Jake misses a high 5 with Andy several times before connecting. Andy stumbles away. Jake collapses on bed with the help of Kyle.]*

KYLE VANDERS: You're alright mate, you're alright. *[Removes the toga and Jake's shoes. He leans in close, and speaks in a whisper]* Don't forget to have a little shoot up before you go to bed, ok?

> *[Jake nods, Kyle returns to his box. Jake stumbles to the desk and rummages through a draw, pulling out a small black bag. He faces his back to the audience for several seconds. When he turns around*

he holds a needle in one hand. He stabs it into his stomach, throws the needle on the desk then collapses on his bed.]

[TIM moves his chair to sit closer to Jake's bed; he has a computer in his lap. Jake continues to lie asleep. Between them is FACEBOOK 2.]

FACEBOOK 2: *[In a overly happy voice]* Tim Hand poked you. *[Pokes Jake]*

[Jake shrieks and sits up rubbing his eyes, Tim sniggers]

FACEBOOK 2: Tim Hand threw a cow at you *[Shoves a stuffed toy at Jake bowling him off the bed. Jake staggers back up]* Tim Hand stuffed ice-cream down your pants *[goes to pull out the front of Jake's pants, Jake slaps him away.*

[Facebook 2 pauses and is joined by FACEBOOK 1.]

FACEBOOK 1: *[Jumps in]* You wish to slap Tim? *[Jake nods. Facebook 1 turns and slaps Tim across the face]* Your slap has been sent.

[Jake collapses back onto the bed only to have his door burst open. Jake is rushed off stage by several people then returned to down stage dressed in lederhosen and a goon box strapped to his head. AMANDA next to him is wearing a bathing suit with green plastic leaves stuck over the breasts and pelvic area, Adam and Eve style. A series of Tableaus follow, in each Tableau Jake and Amanda move closer together. In first Tableau Jake and Amanda are reacting to each other's costumes]

FACEBOOK 7: Kyle Vanders posted a photo in the album 'O-week Drop-Offs'.

FACEBOOK 2: Tim Hand commented on Kyle Vanders photo.

TIM HAND: Dude! WTF. Where are you??

FACEBOOK 1: Comment from Jake Black!

JAKE BLACK: Ok, first of all, I want to say I did NOT dress myself like this. I was ambushed. Seriously mate, would I be wearing THIS if I was lying? According to the college rule book it was expected. I mean, it's definitely expected that your locked door will open at 6am and you'll be held down while some senior collegian uses you as a canvas. It's perfectly normal right?

FACEBOOK 7: Kyle Vanders marked this photo's location as Handorf, local German Town.

> *[Amanda and Jake move into another tableau. Two more people join them. One looks confused and leans in as though to poke Jake's pants, the other stares at his crotch]*

FACEBOOK 6: Courney Gimp posted a photo of you with the caption-

COURTNEY GIMP: The Freshers finally meet the locals.

FACEBOOK 2: Like!

FACEBOOK 4: Comment from Amanda Pickup!

AMANDA PICKUP: OMG. You posted my most embarrassing moment on Facebook!

JAKE BLACK: You've got to give Duncan credit, it took most people ages to realise the lederhosen was painted on and not real clothing.

> *[The person who was poking leaps back in horror. The person staring at the crotch takes a step forward for a closer look. Freeze in new position]*

I think the buckles super glued to my nipples were the main perpetrator of *that* illusion.

FACEBOOK 5: Like!

FACEBOOK 3: Katie Black commented on your photo.

KATIE BLACK: Bro, the look that woman is giving you could peel paint!

FACEBOOK 7: Comment from Kyle Vanders!

KYLE VANDERS: You in time will learn this look, Sister of Jake. Where the parents judge you as the drunken deviant you are and young girls, like yourself, try to take a closer look at your junk.

KATIE BLACK: EEEWWWWW!

JAKE BLACK: *[grins madly]* It was awesome!

KATIE BLACK: Well you're deranged!

[New Tableau, Jake and Amanda realise they have no wallet or phone]

FACEBOOK 7: Kyle Vanders posted a new photo captioned-

KYLE VANDERS: When they finally realised they had no phone or wallet to get back to Adelaide.

FACEBOOK 4: Comment from Amanda Pickup!

AMANDA PICKUP: Kyle you are a lunatic! You realise this, right?

FACEBOOK 1: Jake Black likes Amanda's comment!

JAKE BLACK: Yes… trying to get back without money is not quite as awesome as scaring off young children.

AMANDA PICKUP: Try hitch-hiking when you are with someone who looks like he paints himself rather than buying pants.

[Tableau changes to Jake and Amanda trying to hitchhike]

FACEBOOK 2: Comment from Tim Hand!

TIM HAND: Dude is that a *Goon box* on your head? No wonder the oldies thought you were drunk! Were you playing that Goon of Fortune game I've been hearing about?

FACEBOOK 1: Comment from Jake Black!

JAKE BLACK: So *that's* why they kept driving past!

FACEBOOK 6: Comment!

COURTNEY GIMP: Or because they thought you were spreading the word of the Lord.

FACEBOOK 7: Comment!

KYLE VANDERS: Or because you looked like part of a travelling circus.

FACEBOOK 2: Comment!

TIM HAND: Or because you looked like you were mugged at a yodelling competition.

FACEBOOK 4: Comment!

AMANDA PICKUP: Either way it didn't work!

[Change tableau to Jake and Amanda trying to catch a bus. A DRIVER looks at them with an expression on the tipping point of extreme horror and hysterical laughter]

FACEBOOK 7: Kyle Vanders posted a photo captioned–

KYLE VANDERS: Please explain.

FACEBOOK 6: Comment!

COURTNEY GIMP: That driver's response was a crack up! *[puts on a mocking voice]* "You expect me to believe, that around 50 teenagers are dressed like this every year and dropped off all around Adelaide, without a single fight to keep your clothes on? Without a single hidden dollar up the who-ha?" *[normal voice]* Classic!

FACEBOOK 7: Comment! LOL.

KYLE VANDERS: *[Kyle Vanders starts laughing really hard, and has to calm himself down to speak]* Then he said, "If I see you out here again in anything less than snow gear, I'm going to run you over with this bus."

FACEBOOK 1: Jake Black updated his status!

JAKE BLACK: Does anyone have a good method for removing superglue from skin? *[Points to buckles stuck to nipples]*

> *[Jake returns to his room, puts a shirt and pants on over his lederhosen. Has a couple of beers with ANDY and KYLE.]*

FACEBOOK 1: New status update from Jake Black!

JAKE BLACK: My blood is now 100% beer. So long o-week, and thanks for all the fish!

> *[Collapses on bed, Andy and Kyle return to their boxes. AMANDA appears dressed in jogging gear and stretching.]*

JAKE BLACK: Jake's liver took a beating in college o-week.

AMANDA PICKUP: You want to be a real boy? Go hard or go home Special Boy.

JAKE BLACK: *[Slight groan in voice over as though hung-over]* You're seriously going with Amanda Pickup for your Facebook profile? That's not what your name plate says on your door.

AMANDA PICKUP: A lady has to let the boys know where she stands these days; they don't pick up hints anymore.

[Facebook 5-7 converge on Jake in his room and start bombarding him.]

FACEBOOK 5: Andy Lambert ploughed your field!

[Jake frowns]

FACEBOOK 6: Courtney Gimp stewed your apples!

FACEBOOK 7: Kyle Vanders milked your cows!

FACEBOOK 5-7: *[Chant]* Play FarmVille. Play Farmville. Play Farmville. Play Farmville. Play Farmville.

[Jake screams and flaps the offending Farmville demons away.]

JAKE BLACK: Where were we?

FACEBOOK 4: A lady has to let the boys know where she stands these days; they don't pick up hints

JAKE BLACK: Aha! Us college boys' are pretty awesome, I'm sure you'll find one to your liking. And the walk of shame won't be very far then...

AMANDA PICKUP: *[Tartly]* Just because a girl walks out of college building, dressed in the same clothes as the night before, with her heels in her hand and a bit of sex hair, does not mean she should hurry past the dining hall in shame. I will OWN that walk of shame!

[As Amanda goes to stride past Jake's door, Jake manages to get

off his bed, open his door a crack and watch her go past. Amanda stands on her box again.]

FACEBOOK 7: Kyle Vanders just updated his-

KYLE VANDERS: *[Interjects]* ooohhhhh! Jakey's perving on Amanda!

[Jake makes a rude gesture at Kyle, goes into his room, sits at his desk and sighs.]

FACEBOOK 1: Jake Black updated his status.

JAKE BLACK: is BBBOOOOORRREEEDDDD

[Jake tinkers on the computer for a minute. A murmuring starts in the background. As it gets louder you can make out the words '21 shots of rum'. This continues at a moderate volume. FACEBOOK 1 jumps out with a pirate patch over one eye.]

FACEBOOK 1: Arrrr! Jake now be usin' Ye Olde Facebook in Pirate English.

JAKE BLACK: Hell yeah, boredom averted! *[Sits back to watch the action]*

FACEBOOK 7: Th' infamous landlubber Cap'n Jake now be mateys wit Kyle Vanders n' three other pirates.

ALL: *[uproariously]* 21 shots of rum ago!

FACEBOOK 5: Cap'n Jake be admirin' 'I don't care how comfortable crocs are, you look like a dumbass' an' 5 more scrolls.

GROUP 1: Arr!

GROUP 2: Weigh in!

GROUP 3: Fancy th' Anchor!

FACEBOOK 6: Cap'n Courtney gimp an' 8 scallywags be enjoyin' this.

ALL: 21 shots of rum ago!

FACEBOOK 2: Cap'n Jake an' Cap'n Tim Hand be admirin' 'Jagga Bomb Appreciation Society' an' 'The Drunken Text Appreciation Society'

ALL: 21 shots of rum ago!

GROUP 2: Arr!

GROUP 3: Weigh In!

GROUP 1: Fancy th' Anchor!

FACEBOOK 6: Cap'n Jake an' Cap'n Courtney joined the ship, 'Enjoy it now, because after college it's called alcoholism'.

ALL: Arr! Crew th' ship ye scallywags!

FACEBOOK 4: Cap'n Jake be buryin' treasure at 'Battle of th' Bands'

FACEBOOK 3: Cap'n Jake an' Cap'n Katie Black be admirin' 'The official rules of shotgun'.

ALL: 21 shots of rum ago!

GROUP 3: Arr!

GROUP 1: Weight In!

GROUP 2: Fancy th' Anchor!

FACEBOOK 1: *[Cuts in on the fun]* Jake Black is now using Facebook in English, UK.

[Facebook-ers sigh and return to their stations beside their assigned character. Jake cracks open a beer and sits at his desk.]

JAKE BLACK: Has lost his voice. And is 20.

FACEBOOK 4: Amanda Pickup posted on your wall.

AMANDA PICKUP: Happy b'day. Have an awesome one! See you around, hope you avoid the pond!

JAKE BLACK: *[Jake spurts beer to one side]* What?? I've been wet for like a week; tell me you only get ponded in o-week?

[Amanda stands there grinning.]

FACEBOOK 2: Comment!

TIM HAND: Dude what the fuck is a ponding? P.S. Happy Birthday, Buddy.

FACEBOOK 6: Courtney Gimp commented on your status!

COURTNEY GIMP: A ponding, oh innocent friend of Jake's, is when one picks up the birthday boy or girl and dumps their arse in the courtyard pond.

> *[KYLE and ANDY enter and knock hard on Jake's door. Jake stares at it in comic horror. As Courtney continues to speak, Jake holds onto the door to try and stop the boys from getting in, but is unsuccessful. A struggle ensures]*

COURTNEY GIMP: And if they don't put up a good fight we may do it more than once. In regards to what Amanda said Jake, you WILL NOT avoid the pond. Put up a good fight kiddo.

> *[JAKE gets carried out of his room. KYLE re-enters stage, moves onto his box, without Jake. Jake makes his way back to his room, hair damp, clothes wet. He glares at the computer as Kyle speaks]*

FACEBOOK 7: Kyle Vanders posted on your wall!

Kyle Vanders Hey champ, happy b'day… Nice swim? The best start to a top day! I shall see you at b-ball where we WILL win! *[Spins an imaginary ball on his finger]*

> *[Rest of actors are happily creating a chatting background hum. Jake starts to get ready for Basketball, towelling his hair dry etc]*

KATIE BLACK: Happy birthday!!! Welcome 2 ur last yr as a teenager. Enjoy the last yr that u can justify the risk-taking & irresponsible behaviour. Have a gr8 birthday swim, bro!

JAKE BLACK: *[Jake pauses to type]* First things first: you know how to spell, stop writing like a twelve year old with a pea for a brain. Secondly, thanks. Thirdly… So very, very wet.

> *[Jake pauses, starting at the desk drawer. He shrugs, opens it and pulls out the little black bag. He turns his back to the audience again. Shaking a hand, he turns around sucking his finger, he pulls out a needle, sticks it into his stomach. He cracks his neck, has jump to shake himself out and leaves the room. KYLE stays on box]*

KYLE VANDERS: Whoop, whoop! WINNERS!!!!! *[Mimes lining up a ball and scoring]*

JAKE BLACK: *[Still off stage]* Hypothetical high 5!

> *[JAKE comes into his room with another drink, and collapses happily in his chair.]*

JAKE BLACK: No Mr. Officer, I'm not drunk… I'm just trying to walk like Jack Sparrow. *[In a dream, he reaches into the black bag and uses another needle. Types again.]* Jake is comfortably numb aka smashed. *[Jake appears to sleep in the chair.]*

FACEBOOK 4: Amanda Pickup posted an update.

AMANDA PICKUP: It's 4am and my door knobs missing. WTF!

FACEBOOK 6: Courtney Gimp updated her status.

COURTNEY GIMP: 5 am and only 2 hours and 1000words until this baby needs to be handed in. Come on Red Bull, give me wings!

[Jake opens his eyes and types one fingered.]

FACEBOOK 1: Jake Black is very seedy.

[KATIE, standing tall and wearing 'grandma clothes', speaks in a 'grown up' voice]

KATIE BLACK: Darling, I really hope you are taking care of yourself. With your condition you have to be careful.

[Jake looks confused. Then his face clears.]

JAKE BLACK: Mum, seriously! Get off Katie's account! I can take care of myself.

KATIE BLACK: I know love, I know. But it has only been 6 months and when you're drinking you've got to really watch out.

JAKE BLACK: Stop worrying. I've pricked enough blood to fill a tea cup. I'm fine. How about a happy birthday?

KATIE BLACK: Happy birthday, love.

JAKE BLACK: Next time I'm home we need to set up an FB account for you. Your words next to Katie's name are like looking into a very scary future.

KATIE BLACK: *[Normal voice]* Bite me.

[AMANDA walks on dressed only in a towel with cupcakes on it. She pauses in Jake's doorway.]

AMANDA PICKUP: Hey Jake, going to Australia's Biggest morning Tea?

[Jake turns and freezes, hand raised in an idiotic wave. He manages to nod]

AMANDA PICKUP: Sweet, can't wait to see what you make. *[Waves and sallies off stage]*

[Jake turns back to computer. FACEBOOK 4 jumps onto the stage enthusiastically]

FACEBOOK 4: Jake is attending Australia's Biggest Morning Tea: College.

FACEBOOK 5: Andy Lambert posted on your wall.

ANDY LAMBERT: Coming to Aust biggest MT?

JAKE BLACK: WTF! A on Facebook??

ANDY LAMBERT: Actually, I got attacked by some people and forced to get Facebook. So here I am… woohoo! *[He picks up the black bag from in front of him and pulls out a needle like Jake's. He lifts up the edge of his shorts and sticks it into his thigh.]*

JAKE BLACK: Wicked sick.

ANDY LAMBERT: Getting high on life baby. *[Andy throws needle back into the back.]* So are you coming?

JAKE BLACK: Totally. I baked muffins and everything.

ANDY LAMBERT: What? You're kidding, right?

JAKE BLACK: No, I'm serious. The chicks dig that shit. And I'm a chick magnet, enough said. Have to beat them off with a stick.

[Jake watches the door. He jumps up as AMANDA walks past again and he waves a little too eagerly.]

ANDY LAMBERT: Sure Jakey, blame it on the chicks. Unless you made muffins out of beer, you have just dropped from 'awesome' to 'a little sad' on my cool-o-metre.

JAKE BLACK: And I'm not at 'pathetic' because?

ANDY LAMBERT: We shoot-up together. It redeems you, slightly.

[They both grin and look at their black bags]

JAKE BLACK: It would sound more bad ass if it wasn't insulin, hey?

ANDY LAMBERT: Diabetics go harder!

[Jake lies down on his bed]

FACEBOOK 6: Status update from Courtney Gimp.

COURTNEY GIMP: It's official. Special Boy has broken the Jagga Bomb record, 5 in a row!

FACEBOOK 7: Kyle updated his status.

KYLE VANDERS: Impressed, Jakey managed to play a good game of B-ball after yesterday's Jagga fest.

FACEBOOK 5: Andy Lambert posted on your wall!

ANDY LAMBERT: Keen for a skate?

[With a groan JAKE sits up and goes to sit at his desk. His nose is heavily strapped with tape. He has a dark ring on one eye. ANDY, TIM, AMANDA crowd around Jake on the bed.]

JAKE BLACK: Jake has a broken nose. It hurts.

ANDY LAMBERT: So you did end up breaking your nose? Lol.

AMANDA PICKUP: You know, trying out your usual dance moves on skates wasn't the best idea.

JAKE BLACK: In hindsight skating while seedy, not my best moment. *[goes to rest his face in his hands and pulls back, wincing]*

TIM HAND: Yum, soft foods and liquids! Bet you're loving that.

JAKE BLACK: Bite me.

AMANDA PICKUP: Things could have been worse... you could have sliced off limbs with the blade of your skates...

[Tim, Amanda and Andy back off to their boxes. Andy whispers to FACEBOOK 5 and hands them an envelope. FACEBOOK 5 knocks on Jake's door .]

FACEBOOK 5: *[overly cheerful voice]* Personal message from Andy Lambert to Jake Black.

[Jake takes envelope, and sits at his desk with a groan]

ANDY LAMBERT: Hey Jakey. Are you alright? It's just, you've been seedy a lot mate. I mean don't get me wrong, you do some funny shit when you're hung over; the penguin dive across the ice was epic. But you don't have to go as hardcore as the old blokes at college. They don't really give a shit if you drink like a fish or not.

[Jake massages his temples in agitation then taps the keyboard forcefully]

JAKE BLACK: Thanks for your nosy concern, but for your information I was not drunk when we were skating, I had a flipping low blood sugar level. Alright?

ANDY LAMBERT: *[Pause]* Wanna talk about it?

JAKE BLACK: *[Angry]* About what? The fact that I have to watch everything that I eat? That even watching what I eat isn't enough? Because if I get the carb count wrong and take the wrong dose my blood sugar bounces like a yoyo and I feel shit for days? The fact that I have to plan every inch of my day so there is no room left for any sort of spontaneous activity at all?

ANDY LAMBERT: *[comforting]* I know you're new to this, but I can promise you, from someone who has gone through that shitty learning curve, you get used to it.

JAKE BLACK: I don't want to get *used* to it, Andy! Thinking to myself, I shouldn't eat that, I'll get heart disease. Going from playing b-ball every day to only twice a week because I can't be assed checking my sugar levels before, during and after.

ANDY LAMBERT: I hear you; trying to psych yourself up to inject insulin four times a day is bad enough without having to do it three times a game!

JAKE BLACK: I hate being part of this, this *club*. The diabetics club, where every new person you meet puts in their 2 cents about a friend, cousin, grandparent or neighbour who has it, and how the person they know can't do 'this or that', and am I *sure* I'm allow to do that?

TOGETHER: YES I'M BLOODY SURE!!!

JAKE BLACK: I'm not some old fat geezer who got that way because I didn't look after myself! *[Bursts into tears]*

ANDY LAMBERT: *[light-heartedly]* Then there's the whole issue of trying to look manly while carrying a bag everywhere you go, hey? Damn Target never took needles into consideration when they designed their pockets, the bastards.

[Jake shorts with laughter half-way through his sobs]

There's nothing we can't eat or do we just need to think ahead before we do it.

JAKE BLACK: Before, I didn't have to think about it or plan ahead, I just did it. I'm not like you. Then in two days I went from normal to watching everything I eat, and staring at a needle for twenty minutes trying to convince myself I need it to live. If you don't get it right and go low, you could die, if you don't get it right and go high you damage your organs and end up with one of a hundred extra diseases when you get older. So basically, if you don't get the balance right, you're fucked. And as a newbie you *never* get it right, so you're always fucked. When someone suggests something as simple as going out for a drink or dinner after uni, I want to say yes rather than have to say no every time because I don't have the right insulin with me. I just want to be normal Andy, so all I have to worry about is girls and the fact I'm rooted for exams. That's what happens when you choose the wrong course just so you can get away from your parents.

ANDY LAMBERT: There is no such thing as normal mate. So many people would look at college and say, doing that shit and drinking that much isn't normal.

JAKE BLACK: Drinking is something I can control, if I know it's coming and I can just be like every other happy go lucky dickhead out there. Diabetes doesn't *own* me. I plan ahead now, not to avoid dying, but so I can live!

ANDY LAMBERT: When I first found out I had it, I was pissed off at everyone. It took me a good 6 months to realise it wasn't going away and I wasn't helping anyone by being angry, least of all myself. It's a conscious decision you have to make. But don't forget, I'm here for ya mate.

JAKE BLACK: Thanks.

[Jake sighs, and fetches a large pile of papers onto his desk. Starts

looking all over his room, bitting his nails, and doing anything other than looking at the papers.]

JAKE BLACK: Is shitttttt bored. *[Pauses for a moment, sighs]* Is studying.

[TIM enters stage, all rugged up with a beanie and scarf]

FACEBOOK 2: Tim Hand posted on Jake Black's Wall!

TIM HAND: While you're procrastinating, I'm overseas tomorrow!! NZ here I come!!

JAKE BLACK: Hope your ski rebounds off a rock and flicks you in the nuts.

TIM HAND: No need to be like that, Jakey. We can't all be stuck in the books like you.

[AMANDA busts into JAKE's room holding two fake guitars]

AMANDA PICKUP: Bored?

JAKE BLACK: Jake is guitar heroing it up!

[Jake and Amanda start to play guitar hero in the room. There is a hum in the background made up by the arrayed characters who are 'on Facebook'. Jake and Amanda collapse in a heap laughing. Jake leans in and kisses her. Amanda and Jake pull apart. Amanda, all coy, points to the papers and then leaves. Jake sits at his desk with a big grin]

FACEBOOK 2: Comment from Tim Hand!

TIM HAND: We should probably date.

JAKE BLACK: *[startled out of his daydream]* What do you mean 'we'?

TIM HAND: With women you retard.

JAKE BLACK: Owch, way to assume I'm as retarded as you!

TIM HAND: Jake, I've never seen anyone less of a player then you. There's no way you've scored already.

[Tim leaves. Jake plays with paper and becomes more panicky]

JAKE BLACK: Jake is 4 and a half hours away from freedom/ intoxication. *[Riffles through paper frantically]* 4 hours…

[Before Jake rushes out the door he turns and types. FACEBOOK 1 jumps into the room]

FACEBOOK 1: Jake joined the group Next semester I'm going to study from the beginning. *[Starts pointing people out in the crowd]* You should probably join to. Oh, and you. And you, yes you, you definitely look like a slacker. Another Facebook group should do you good.

[Andy and Jake both leave the stage]

FACEBOOK 5: Status update from Andy Lambert. This exam is going to be awesome thanks to my handy faculty-approved cheat sheet!

FACEBOOK 1: Status update from Jake Black. Holy shit! We were allowed flipping cheat sheets! Why didn't anyone tell me!

FACEBOOK 5: Status update from Andy Lambert. That test was easier then letting rip after some baked beans.

FACEBOOK 1: Status update from Jake Black. Answer to Question 4 – Picture of an elephant. Perhaps I'll get sympathy marks for my artistic ability.

[JAKE returns and throws his bag on the bed. He scoops up several beer bottles]

FACEBOOK 1: Jake Black posted a new status update!

JAKE BLACK: Jake is getting intoxicated.

[Dances out of the room. Several Tableaus of him partying, initially standing up and as the tableaus progress he gets closer and closer to the ground. He returns to his room, stumbling. He drops empty bottles across his desk.]

FACEBOOK 1: Jake updated his status!

JAKE BLACK: Is seedy.

[He reaches for his black bag and with much fumbling, manages to prick his finger in view of the audience and press it against a small machine. He picks up a needle from the bag but drops it under the bed. He types]

JAKE BLACK: Is still seedy.

[He lies on the floor and reaches under the bed groping blindly. When he doesn't find it he lets his head drop to the floor and closes his eyes. Jake remains still on his floor.]

KYLE VANDERS: *[Eating from a bowl]* Yo, Jakey you missed breakfast. Went hard did ya mate?

ANDY LAMBERT: Dude you're 20 mins late. 5 more mins then I'm busting the door on your arse. I don't care if you're naked!

[Kyle and Andy march over to Jake's door. After trying the doorknob several times and knocking, Kyle leaves and returns with a set of keys. They unlock the door to find Jake on the ground. They go through the motions of tying to wake him up. Andy rushes to the black bag but finds it empty. They call emergency services and the stage lights on Jake's room go out. FACEBOOK

3 with a white envelope wanders around the stage and Jake's room looking lost. It stands uncertainly in the middle of Jake's room]

FACEBOOK 3: [*Uncertain and lost*] Personal message for Jake Black from Katie Black. Message subject: Now what have you done?

[A pacing KATIE enters stage left. She is angry.]

KATIE BLACK: Dickhead! You said you would look after yourself! You said you'd be careful! When you get out of your coma I'm going to wring your neck for scaring the shit out of me!

[Katie walks through Jake's door and sits on the bed staring blankly ahead.]

KATIE BLACK: You didn't move. I sang to you for hours and you didn't move. Come back Jakey. Please.

[After staring into space collapses on the floor]

KATIE BLACK: Love you forever.

[Katie leaves stage. TIM, AMANDA, COURTNEY, ANDY and KYLE are arrayed in a semi-circle on stage. Kyle looks crushed, and Andy sits in a ball on the floor gripping his black bag tight. The other three are typing away unconcerned, at their laptops sitting on their knees. Kyle finally takes a deep breath and types]

KYLE VANDERS: Rest peacefully mate.

[Tim, Amanda and Courtney all stiffen, looking at the computer in disbelief]

AMANDA PICKUP: [*Stands up and moves into Jake's room*] Miss you terribly Jake...Will never forget your whacky dancing or our guitar hero sessions... You were special to all of us at college; we're going to miss you so, so much. No one will ever replace you. *[She slowly collapses at the foot of Jake's Bed]*

COURTNEY GIMP*:* I don't know what to say. You always had so much energy and a crazy appetite for high five's. Your last name always made me laugh because you were white as an albino and had hair a blond could be proud of. You were pretty much the only person I would stop and talk to on the way to uni, because you always had some epic story to share.

TIM HAND: Jakey... *[Pauses, overcome.]* Sorry mate, I have only just started to believe it and plucked up the courage to write this message on your wall. I'm still overseas and I had to find out through Facebook. God, that hurt. You were always there to brighten the day and see the funny side of everything. Wish we could turn back that clock, eh? Hope you were ripping it up in Adelaide cause I haven't seen you since you left, man. See you in the next life buddy.

ANDY LAMBERT: *[In anguish, frequent pauses]* Mate, I really miss you. I think of you every day. I wish I could have done more, thought to check sooner, and I'm so sorry you're gone. I'll remember you always; you were one in a million. There is a memorial service this Friday; I will be there for sure. Your diabetic buddy, Andy... Don't forget 'diabetics go harder', *[whispers]* miss you mate.

> *[KATIE walks into his room. She closes his laptop, picks up Jake's suitcase and leaves. FACEBOOK 5 enters stage with a white envelope and wanders, lost, as they speak.]*

FACEBOOK 5: Personal Message from Andy Lambert to Jake Black. Message subject: I can't believe it's been a year.

ANDY LAMBERT: Hey mate, haven't been on Facebook much lately. Just been taking this semester off, taking it easy. Not at college anymore, had enough of all that last year and moved out. Try to keep up with people. *[Pauses, serious]* Still have nightmares. And I still miss you, mate.

[Stage to black]

END

Enjoyed Jake's Page?

Why not check out other Facebook Novels by this author?

The Grand Adventures of Madeline Cain
Available at all online book and ebook retailers.

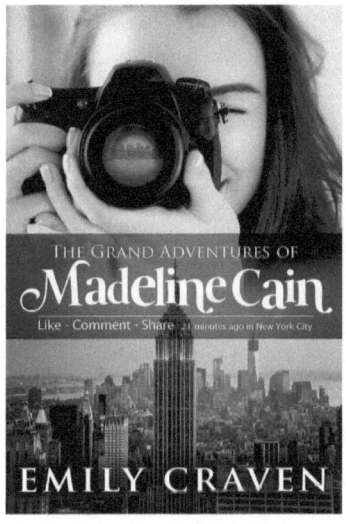

Newsfeed [Share your thoughts]

Madeline Cain Photographer Extraordinaire Put this on your status if you know someone (or are related to someone) who has been eaten by dragons. Dragons are nearly unstoppable and in case you didn't know, they can breathe fire. 93% of people won't copy and paste this, because they have already been eaten by dragons. The other 7% are sitting in the shower armed with fire extinguishers. *Posted 15 hours ago* [Comment . Like]

Madeline has achieved her dream, acceptance into world famous photographer, Jason I'Anson's, exclusive college in New York. Like many people of her generation who travel overseas, she turns to Facebook as a medium to pass on news and keep in touch with her family and friends. But her move from the sleepy Australian town of Adelaide to New York City doesn't exactly turn out as she expected. From her first meeting with her chain smoking, club crazy house mate and his superhero Mexican Chameleon, Duncan (who can move from one side of the room to the other in a blink of eye), she knew she was in for an interesting time. Add an umbrella rigged by her brother to yell abuse at surrounding pedestrians when it rains, pizza deliveries to porn sets and being pulled in by the FBI for questioning after an explorative stint into spy photography, and things move from the interesting to the ridiculous.

Egged on by her Australian Facebook friends, Kathy the hypochondriac and Tim, who has a strange sexual affinity for electrical appliances, Madeline tries to find her feet in the big city. But this may be harder for her to achieve than first thought, after she accidentally blackmails a famous model cheating on her boyfriend.

In a world of status updates, blogs and photographic file sharing, where everyone who adds you can follow your every move, how the hell is Madeline supposed to get out of the hole she found herself in?

Get It Now!

Seek Peek Of The Grand Adventures of Madeline Cain: Photographer Extraordinaire

NOTES > My Notes   [Write a note]

Who Owns a Chameleon? Seriously??

By **Madeline Cain The Great**. Wednesday, 2 January 2012 at 04:00.

Just wanted to say, this wasn't how I imagined the start of my grand adventure; a prig for a housemate and some unidentifiable (possibly Mexican) amphibian called Duncan.

My vision of studio loft apartments, spacious and bright come nowhere close to describing this disturbing student housing. I mean, I'm paying a fortune, I have to find a job, and all I get is some crummy, two bedroom apartment with paint peeling off the walls, a cupboard for a kitchen and a bathroom that makes a moss infested cave network look like a barren desert plain. Seriously, there is enough mould on those tiles to start producing our own penicillin tablets.

They have put me in the same apartment as some random guy called Kim. How was I supposed to know that Kim was a guy's name? Perhaps the College, rather than asking if I wanted to room with Kim Enuik, should have asked if I minded rooming with a growth stunted, lean, chain-smoking, scarf-wearing metro GUY. If first impressions are an indicator of the year to come, then this year is going to be more *interesting* and less *exciting* than I planned.

My first meeting with Kim and Duncan started with me kicking my bedroom door down. After the fifth kick the door flew open and I dropped my bags in the bare, 3m squared room.

"Holy shit." That's all I could say. "Holy shit holy shit holy shit holy shit."

It was delightfully decorated with dusty metal blinds, carpet stains of an unknown nature, one wooden desk and a single bed. The mattress was an uninviting light green, and appeared to have a misshapen lump at its core.

"What a shit hole," I muttered. Exhausted, I went to lie on the bed, misshapen or not.

"GRRRRRRRRRRRRRR....."

I leapt backward flattening myself against the opposite wall as the mattress ceased to sound like a Koala deprived of its gum leaf drugs. Approaching the bed again I saw two eyes blinking lazily amongst the green. On closer inspection I could identify the outline of a long four-legged, spiky-tailed lizard exactly the same colour as the bloody bed!

"Hola!" growled the apparition.

"Bloody hell!" I mashed myself against the wall, body turning to seek escape through the open door. Only to be stopped short by Kim, bored eyes watching me.

"So you've met Duncan?"

"Hola!" came the low growl from the bed.

I liked my dry lips and asked, "What the hell is that?"

"What does it look like? It's a fricken Chameleon."

"Oh."

Kim continued to stare in distain. "Don't they have zoos in the UK?"

I drew myself up. "UK? I'm not a Pom, I'm Australian."

"Aren't you used to big f-off Alligators then? A Chameleon's the purring cat of reptiles, I thought you Aussies had more balls."

God that bloke got under my skin quicker than an alien probe. "Look mate I'm from Adelaide, it's a city with over a million people, not the middle of Whoop-Whoop."

"A million people and you think this…Adelaide, is a city?"

"Well in comparison to… but we still have a… I mean we don't have any flipping…. Look, who the hell are you?"

He lifted one well groomed eyebrow. "Kim, I live here."

"But you're a guy." Yeah, I know, enter Captain Obvious.

"Well spotted genius. Next you'll be telling me Duncan's a lizard."

Flicking his fringe like a well rehearsed Panteen ad, he sauntered through, picked up the two and a half foot-long Duncan and returned to the door. As Duncan slowly discarded green for navy blue to merge with Kim's vest, Kim paused and looked over his shoulder like a character in a bad Australian Soapie.

"Duncan is a very rare and valuable pet. Under no circumstances are you to feed him and if you give him an avenue to escape you'll wish you stayed in Kangaroo land. If you can follow these rules then we will get along just fine. Welcome to student housing."

What the hell!! Just because he wears a scarf and smokes like a chimney does not make him better than me! Christ, I wear a scarf because it flipping minus seven degrees and snowing!

He is the strangest, most predictable character I have ever met. Kim divides his time between four locations: a) his precious NYU where he studies promotion and marketing, b) his bed room, more often than not climbing onto the fire-escape outside his window to smoke, c) making microwave oven meals in the kitchen and d) interning at one of NY's hottest night clubs in Soho, The Dragon's Den.

I have been here less than three days and I have found Duncan in no less than fifty different places in the apartment, waiting to scare the living daylights out of me. He's like Speedy Gonzales on steroids dressed in camouflage armour. He's like the superman of lizards. You never see him move, he vanishes and reappears from one end of the room to the other in seconds and he is indestructible. Hola! Next to my head in the morning. Hola! Materialising on the sink when I spit out tooth paste. Hola! In my yet to be unpacked suitcase this morning. Hola! Hola! Hola! Hola!

This could be worse than the prospect of one day rooming with Tim and his abnormal sexual fetish for electrical appliances.

Anyway, that's beside the point, I'm angry, I'm jetlagged and I've got to de-Duncan my room before I enter zombie like slumber.

[Comment . Like . Share]

Harry Lee and **3 others** like this.

Nadine Cain Darling that's horrible! Are there at least two dead bolts on your door? You don't have to stay honey. Come home. I found this lovely photography course for you at Uni SA, lots of knowledgeable instructors and a very good reputation. Daddy and I can convert the new study back into your old room like that! *Posted 1hr ago* [Comment . Like]

Nadine Cain Oh Maddie, I don't mean to sound like a nag but next time please call us to let us know you're safe, a note on Facebook two days after you arrived is just inconsiderate. Love you. Xoxoxoxox. *Posted 1hr 2mins ago* [Comment . Like]

Madeline Cain The Great Mum I did not spend three hours

with you on the computer setting up your account, adding your friends and showing you how to message me and view my posts so that I could waste a billion dollars calling Australia from a payphone. When I finally stumble out to see the sights I'll buy a calling card. And Jason is my idol! I am NOT going to Uni SA to study; it's super hard to get into I'Anson Photographic College. Nice try though. Love ya. *Posted 12 hrs ago* [Comment . Like]

Kathy Bloomingdale Wow Mad, that sounds full on! Hopefully once the jetlag dust settles and you start your course with Jason you'll feel a million bucks. Please put up pictures of Duncan. I've never seen a Chameleon before! How exciting! And after that toaster, burnt bread, knife incident I really think we should reconsider moving in with Tim next year. I mean the butterflies are off putting enough.... *Posted 5 hrs ago* [Comment . Like]

About The Author

Chocolate. Karaoke. Star Trek. Travel. Books. Puppies. Shaking what your Mama gave you. All of these are some of my favourite things. But when I meet someone, I want to know who they are, not what they like. I want to know what's their story? Why do they get up every morning? Other than, like, needing to have a pee.

Aherm, moving on.

For me, what rocks my world is showing daring creatives how to draw the curious down the rabbit hole with stories, how to use their tales to spark connection, understanding, and create belonging with a wonderland of their making.

Stories entered my DNA as a kid. They were what saved me from lonely lunch times with no friends when my family moved states and I was shoved into a new school mid-year, mid-puberty, mid-awkward-phase. They allowed me to escape to another world of adventure, of struggle (that wasn't mine), of empathy, perspective, and heroes who strived against the bullies, and again and again, picked themselves. Stories showed me how to adapt, to care, to trust myself. They understood me on a level I barely understood myself. I was such a voracious reader I started writing my own books when I was 12 because my favourite authors just couldn't keep up.

Stories were how I survived boredom. Boredom was how I ended up a Star Trek nerd. Every afternoon when I got home from school, my mother commandeered the TV to fuel her Star Trek addiction. The choice was be bored or be obsessed. You could say I was brain-washed a Trekkie and I have no regrets!

That's the only reason I can think of for how I ended up choosing to study Astrophysics. Two years in and something happened that I never in a million years expected. I hated it. I had no idea what else I would even do if I quit. I was good at it, sure, but every six months I would have a mini-break-down in my bedroom, the words of high-school teachers and parents going around and round my head – 'you're too smart for art.' If present me could time travel, I'd go back and slap them all up-side the head, with a loud, 'fuck that noise' for good measure.

How many times have you been told you 'should'? You should do this, you should do that, even though you know that box doesn't fit you?

What I didn't realise at the time was the reason I was so drawn to Star Trek wasn't the science, it was the adventure. A soap opera in space; people working together solving problems, falling in love, and shooting phasers! This was the root of my unhappiness; I was suppressing the biggest part of myself. I didn't want knowledge for the sake of knowledge, I want to create things that connected people. And the way that excited me, that lit a fire in my belly to create that connection, was by creating and sharing stories. Fictional preferably, with a hint of magic, a dash of quirky, and a sneaky side of truth.

I wish I could tell you that when I set my sights on career as storyteller, I shook off that 'should' energy. I did not. While I devoured dozens of courses on writing, publishing, marketing, editing and eBooks, and learnt one of the most important lessons of my life – that what you create alone will never be as good as what you'll create together with the feedback of professionals who aren't you and see your blind spots – I was still doing all the things you should. You should send your novels to traditional publishers, you should write short stories to get a name for yourself, you should have a 'very' professional website where you're 'very serious' and therefore 'competent', as confirmed by your head shot which makes you look like you have sat on a cactus.

I waited a really long time for someone to pick me. And I was lonely, so very very lonely. When a boy who already had a 3-book deal with a major publisher got the only writing grant available in the state to writers under 30, something finally snapped for me. I was sick of waiting; it was time to choose myself. I couldn't be rejected if I was the one creating the thing, right?

It was when I took the conscious decision to step off the beaten path that things changed for me. I created my own opportunities, but in a way that no one else was doing at the time – I created them so that I was making and creating WITH someone else. The power of collaboration runs through everything I do now, from the very first writing and publishing project I created in my little city of Adelaide, which spiralled into a 5-year international endeavour that would turn into the award-winning storytelling app, Story City, and lift up over 300 storytellers across half a dozen creative industries.

In creating my own opportunities, in making things like Story City, my novels, my branding work, I realised I made a place where I belonged, and where hundreds and thousands of others realised they belonged.

The success that I have had today is due largely to the power of story. Of how stories allow you to be understood for you, and to connect beyond yourself. I've won awards, presented hundreds of hours of storytelling workshops internationally, published 6 books, edited and/or published dozens of authors, I am a global entrepreneur of an app that helps you explore and connect to a city and the stories of its people, and I'm part of a 6 person team that brands a handful of high-flying femmpreneurs every year.

While much of that has been because of hard work, talent, and practice, the truth of the matter is I have gotten this far because I have chosen to make things together, rather than alone. To hone my understanding, skills and stories, with outside eyes, because through collaboration I make far more impact than I ever would on my own.

So I say to you pick yourself, don't wait for others to pick you. But also pick doing it together, rather than doing it alone.

Find your people. Band together. And you will make great things.

Contact Emily Online

Facebook: *http://www.facebook.com/EmilyCravenAuthor*

Website (bookmark me!): *http://www.cravenstories.com*

Twitter: *@cravenstories*

Instagram: *@imagesforjoy*

Email: emily (at) cravenstories (dot) com

Jake's Page Cover Design
By Kit Forster Design

Website: https://www.literartydesign.com/